BEST AUSSIE JOKES

Published by Brolga Publishing Pty Ltd
ABN 46 063 962 443
PO Box 12544
A'Beckett St
Melbourne, VIC, 8006
Australia

email: markzocchi@brolgapublishing.com.au

Copyright © 2014 Marguerite Marshall
National Library of Australia Cataloguing-in-Publication
        Marshall, Marguerite
        Best Aussie jokes : how to be the life of the party
        9781922175557 (paperback)
        Australian wit and humor.
        A828.02

Printed in Australia
Cover design & Typesetting by Brolga Publishing

BE PUBLISHED

Publish through a successful publisher. National distribution, Macmillan & International distribution to the United Kingdom, North America. Sales Representation to South East Asia
Email: markzocchi@brolgapublishing.com.au

BEST AUSSIE JOKES

HOW TO BE THE LIFE OF THE PARTY

MARGUERITE MARSHALL

INTRODUCTION

My mother loved to tell a good joke. So that's how it began for me. But this book probably started when a good friend regaled us with jokes, one after another after another, at a dinner party. Not to be outdone I started trying to remember jokes and give her as good as I got.

Then I have some very witty friends, who share their jokes, which I can't resist sending to other friends to enjoy. So for more than ten years we have shared chuckles primarily via emails.

Thanks to all you funny people, too many to name, for bringing laughter to my life. I hope those who read this book will not only enjoy themselves, but will be able to find a joke for every occasion - well almost! The jokes are sorted alphabetically in categories - so just dip in.

MARGUERITE MARSHALL

ACCIDENTS

An old man lay sprawled across three seats in the picture theatre.

When the usher came by and noticed this, he whispered to the old man,

"Sorry sir, but you're only allowed one seat."

The old man just groaned but didn't budge. The usher became impatient.

"Sir, if you don't get up I'll have to call the manager." Once again, the old man just groaned.

The usher marched briskly back up the aisle, and shortly returned with the manager.

Together the two of them repeatedly tried to move the old dishevelled man, but with no success.

Finally, they summoned the police.

The officer surveyed the situation briefly then asked, "All right mate what's your name?"

"Fred," the old man moaned.

"Where ya from, Fred?" asked the police officer.

With terrible pain in his voice, and without moving a muscle, Fred replied,

"The balcony."

★

Geoff fell from the roof while cleaning the gutters and sustained concussion and several broken bones.

On awakening he found himself in a Catholic Hospital. As he improved a nun asked him how he was going to pay for his treatment.

She asked if he had health insurance?

"No," Geoff whispered.

The nun asked, "Do you have money to pay for the treatment?"

He replied, "No money in the bank."

The nun asked, "Do you have a relative who could pay for you?"

Geoff said, "I've only got a spinster sister, who is a nun." The nun took umbrage at that and said loudly, "Nuns are not spinsters!

We are married to God."

Geoff replied, "Then ask my brother-in-law to pay."

ADVENTURE

Two old friends met regularly for a chat and sat on their favourite bench in the local park. One day when the nearby community hall was being used for a flower show, Betty leant over and said to her friend Myrtle, "You know Myrtle, I've never done anything outrageous in my life."

"Oh dear, Betty," said Myrtle, "If you're going to do something, you've got to do it now."

Betty said, "Good idea." She took off her clothes and streaked through the hall. On her return looking flushed and cheerful, Myrtle asked how she went.

"It was great!" said Betty. "I won first prize in dried arrangements."

AEROPLANES

Ireland's worst air disaster occurred early this morning when a small two-seater Cessna plane crashed into a cemetery. Irish search and rescue workers have recovered 1,826 bodies so far and expect that number to climb as digging continues into the night.

AFGHANI

After years of Western military presence in Afghanistan an Australian female journalist who had written about female oppression under the Taliban regime was sent back there by her newspaper to find out how the status of women had improved.

She was shocked to see that women still walked several paces behind their husbands after the overthrow of the Taliban and years of war.

The journalist interviewed several Afghani women and asked, "Although the Taliban oppressive regime to women has been defeated, why are you still walking several paces behind your husbands?"

A woman smiled and answered, "Land mines."

AGES

Several girlfriends in their 40s discussed where they should meet for dinner. Finally, it was agreed that they should meet at the Ocean View restaurant because the waiters there wore tight pants.

Ten years later in their 50s, the friends again discussed where they should meet for dinner. Finally they decided to meet at the Ocean View restaurant because the food and wine selections were very good.

Ten years later in their 60s, the women again discussed where they should meet for dinner. They finally agreed that they should meet at the Ocean View restaurant because they could eat there in peace and quiet and the restaurant had a beautiful ocean view.

Ten years later in their 70s, the group yet again discussed where they should meet for dinner. Finally it was agreed that they should meet at the Ocean View restaurant because the restaurant was wheel chair accessible and had an elevator.

Ten years later in their 80s, the friends again discussed where they should meet for dinner. Finally it was agreed that they should meet at the Ocean View restaurant because they had never been there before.

ANIMALS

A circus owner runs an ad for a lion tamer and two people show up. One is Bret a retired footballer in his sixties and the other is Melinda a gorgeous blonde in her twenties. The circus owner tells them, "I'm not going to sugar coat it. This is a ferocious lion. He ate my last tamer, so you two had better be good or you're history. Here's your equipment – chair, whip and a gun. Who wants to try out first?"

Melinda says, "I'll go first." She walks past the chair, the whip, and the gun, and steps right into the lion's cage. The lion starts to snarl and pant and begins to charge her. About halfway there, she throws open her coat revealing her beautiful body.

The lion stops dead in his tracks, sheepishly crawls up to her and starts licking her feet and ankles. He continues to lick and kiss her entire body for several minutes and then rests his head at her feet.

The circus owner's jaw is on the floor. He says, "I've never seen a display like that in my life." He then turns to Bret and asks, "Can you top that?"

The tough old footballer replies, "No problem, just get that lion out of there."

★

Jake the son of a sheep station owner from outback Western Australia is sent to university, but halfway through the semester he's squandered all his money.

He calls his dad and says, "You won't believe what modern education is developing...they actually have a program here in Perth that will teach our dog Dundee how to talk."

"That's amazing!" his dad says. "How do I get Dundee in that program?"

"Just send him down here with $2,000," Jake says, "and I'll get him in the course."

So his father sends the dog and $2,000.

About halfway through the semester, the money runs out again. Jake calls his dad.

"So how's Dundee doing, son?" his father wants to know.

"Awesome Dad, he's talking and is the best in his class. But you won't believe this. The uni's had such good results with talking, they've begun to teach the animals how to read!"

"Read?" exclaims his father. "No kidding! How do we get Dundee in that program?"

"Just send $3,000. I'll get him in the class."

The money promptly arrives. But Jake has a problem. At the end of the year, his father will find out the dog can neither talk nor read.

So he shoots the dog. When he arrives home at the end of the year, his father is very excited.

"Where's Dundee? I just can't wait to talk with him and see him read something!"

"Dad," Jake says, "I've some bad news. Last night, Dundee was in the living room, in his special arm chair, reading the West Australian. Then he turned to me and asked, 'So, is your dad still bonking that blonde barmaid at the pub?'" The father groans and whispers, "I hope you shot that b******** before he talks to your Mother!"

★

A vampire bat returned to the cave at night with his face dripping with fresh blood and parked himself on the roof to get some sleep.

Soon the bats in the cave smelled the blood and crowded around him wanting to know where he got it.

He told them to leave him alone and let him get some sleep, but they continued badgering him until he finally gave in.

"Alright, follow me", he said and flew out of the cave with hundreds of excited bats behind him.

Up a mountain they flew and down the other side and eventually into an enormous forest.

Finally the bat slowed down and the others excitedly milled around him, tongues hanging out for blood.

"Do you see that large oak tree over there?" he asked.

"YES, YES, YES!" the bats screamed in a frenzy.

"Good for you." said the bat, "Because I didn't!"

ARABIAN

The son of an Arab sheikh attends school in England.

After a while he writes to his father the sheikh. "England is nice and everyone is friendly and school is good. But I'm ashamed to arrive at school in my gold Rolls Royce when the other students arrive by train."

A week later, he receives a letter from his father, with a blank cheque saying, "Don't shame us. Buy a train too."

ARMED FORCES

A tough old Sergeant Major found himself at a university gala event. Many young idealistic women attended the event and one started speaking with him.

"Excuse me, Sergeant Major, but you seem to be a very serious man. Is something bothering you?" she asked.

"Negative, ma'am. Just serious by nature."

The young woman looked at his awards and decorations and said, "You've seen a lot of action."

"Yes, ma'am, a lot of action."

The young woman, tiring of trying to start up a conversation, said, "You know, you should lighten up. Relax and enjoy yourself."

The Sergeant Major just stared at her in his serious manner.

Finally the young lady said, "You know, I hope you don't take this the wrong way, but when is the last time you had sex?"

"1955, ma'am."

"Well, that's why you're so serious. You really need to chill out! I mean, no sex since 1955!"

She took his hand and led him to a private room where she proceeded to "relax" him several times.

Afterwards, panting for breath, she leaned against his bare chest and said, "Wow, you sure didn't forget much since 1955."

The Sergeant Major said, after glancing at his watch, "I hope not; it's only 2130 now."

★

In 1964 John Henderson was conscripted to fight in Vietnam. On the first morning the army issued him with a brush and comb. That afternoon they shaved his hair off.

The next morning they issued Henderson with a toothbrush and toothpaste. Then that afternoon they removed his lower teeth. The third morning the army issued him with a jockstrap. Henderson failed to appear for lunch duty and the army is still searching for him.

ATHEISTS

An atheist was walking through the woods. "What magnificent trees! What an enormous river! What colourful birds," he marvelled.

Suddenly, he heard a rustling in the bushes behind him.

He turned around... and saw an eight foot grizzly bear charging towards him.

The atheist tore as fast as he could along the path.

He looked over his shoulder and saw that the bear was

closing in on him.

He looked over his shoulder again, and the bear was even closer... and then... the atheist tripped and fell.

Rolling over to pick himself up, he found the bear was right on top of him... reaching towards him with its left paw... and raising the right paw to strike.

At that instant the atheist cried out,

"Oh God help!"

Time stopped...

The bear froze...

The forest was silent...

A bright light shone upon the man, and a voice came out of the sky...

"You deny my existence for all these years, you tell others I don't exist and even credit creation to cosmic accident... Do you expect me to help you out of this predicament? Am I to count you as a believer?"

The atheist looked directly into the light...

"It would be hypocritical of me to suddenly ask you to treat me as a Christian now... but perhaps you could make the bear a Christian?"

... a pause ...

"Very well," said the voice...

The light went out.

The sounds of the forest resumed...

And the bear dropped his right arm...

brought both paws together...

bowed his head and spoke...

"For what I am about to receive may the Lord make me truly thankful."

AUSTRALIAN

Three Aussie blokes Curley, Coot and Bluey are working on a mobile 'phone tower when they knock off for a smoko.

As they descend, Coot slips, falls off the tower and dies instantly.

As the ambulance takes the body away, Bluey says, "Blimey, someone's gotta tell Coot's missus."

Curley says, "OK, I'm pretty good at that sensitive stuff. I'll do it."

Two hours later, he comes back carrying a slab of beer. Bluey says, "Where'd you get the grog, Curley?"

"Coot's wife gave it to me," Curley replies.

"Well blow me down. You told the Missus her hubby was dead and she gave you a slab of beer?"

"Well, not exactly," Curley says. "When she answered the door, I said to her, "You must be Coot's widow.""

She said, "You must be mistaken... I'm not a widow." Then I said, "I'll betcha a slab of beer you are..."

★

Larry a wealthy man in Florida was famous for his parties. One evening, his guests were enjoying themselves as usual – dancing, eating superb seafood, drinking champagne. Then Larry announced that before the party he had a four metre long alligator placed in his pool. "I'll give half a million dollars to anyone who has the nerve to jump in," he dared. Just then there was an almighty splash and Fred the Aussie was fighting the alligator. Fred was punching and jabbing the alligator's eyes, head butting, kicking and biting him. Then he straddled the alligator and encircled his neck squeezing with all his might. The man and animal flipped round and round amid gushes of water, showering the goggle-eyed party goers. Groans and shrieks escaped from Fred and the alligator frantically thrashed the pool. Then suddenly it stopped and the corpse floated on top, while Fred painfully dragged himself out of the pool.

And lay down. Larry rushed up to him. "Fred you're marvellous. You've earned your half a million."

"Don't bother," said Fred. "I don't want it."

"What? Fred, what do you mean? I've got to reward you. How about a house then?"

"No. Really, I don't want it."

"How about a Rolls?"

"No. There's only one thing I want."

"Tell me. Anything."

"Who was the son of a b.... who pushed me in?!"

★

An Australian tour guide was showing a group of American tourists the Top End. On their way to Kakadu the guide described the amazing abilities of the Australian Aborigines to track man or beast over land, through the air and under the sea. The Americans were incredulous. Later that day, as the group rounded a bend on the highway they discovered an Aborigine lying flat in the middle of the road... with one ear pressed to the white line. The bus stopped and the guide and the tourists gathered around the prostrate Aborigine...

"Hey Jacky," said the tour guide, "what are you tracking and what are you listening for?" The Aborigine replied, "Down the road about 25 kilometres is a 1971 Valiant Ute... It's a red one...

the left front tyre is bald... the front end is out of whack, and him got bloody dents in every panel... There are seven black fellas in the back, all drinking beer. Two kangaroos on the roof rack and three dogs on front seat."

The American tourists moved forward, astounded by this precise and detailed knowledge. "Good Lord man, how do you know all that?" asked one.

The Aborigine replied, "I fell out of the bloody thing about half an hour ago!"

BABIES

With all the advances in modern medicine, a 67-year-old friend of mine was able to give birth.

When she was discharged from the hospital and went home, I paid a visit.

"May I see the new baby?" I asked.

"Not yet," she said. "I'll make coffee and we can chat first."

Half an hour passed, and I asked, "May I see the bub now?"

"No, not yet," she said.

After another while, I asked again, 'May I see the baby now?'

"No, not yet," replied my friend.

Growing very impatient, I asked, 'Well, when can I see the baby?'

"When he cries!" she said.

"When he cries?" I said.

"Why?"

"BECAUSE I FORGOT WHERE I PUT HIM, OK?"

★

A pregnant woman was in a bad car accident, then fell into a deep coma. After nearly six months, she awoke and saw that she was no longer pregnant. Frantically, she asks the doctor about her baby.

The doctor replies, "Ma'am, you had twins – a boy and a girl. The babies are fine. Your brother came in and named them."

The woman thinks, "Oh, no! Not Ted; he's an idiot!"

Nervously, she asks the doctor, "What's the girl's name?"

"Denise," the doctor answers.

The new mother thinks, "Oh! That's a beautiful name, maybe I was wrong about Ted. I really like the name Denise."

"What's the boy's name?"

The doctor replies, "Denephew."

★

Q: Should I have a baby after 40?
A: No, 40 children are enough.

Q : Do I have to have a baby shower?
A: Not if you change the baby's nappy very quickly.

BARBECUE

Each Friday night after work, Max would fire up the barbie in his backyard and cook some steak.

All of Max's neighbours were Catholic and as it was Lent, they were forbidden from eating meat on a Friday. The delicious aroma from the grilled steaks wafted over the neighbourhood and was causing such a problem for the Catholic faithful that they finally talked to their priest.

The priest visited Max and suggested that he become a Catholic. After several classes and much study, Max attended Mass and as the priest sprinkled holy water over him, he said,

"You were born a Lutheran and raised a Lutheran but now you are a Catholic." Max's neighbours were relieved, until Friday night arrived and the wonderful aroma of grilled beef filled the neighbourhood again.

They called the priest immediately and he rushed to Max's preparing to scold him. On arrival he stopped and watched in amazement. Max was clutching a small bottle of holy water, which he carefully sprinkled over the grilling meat while saying: "You wuz born a cow, you wuz raised a cow but now you is a flathead."

BATTLE OF THE SEXES

A woman arrived at the Gates of Heaven. While she waited for Saint Peter to greet her, she peeked through the gates. She saw a beautiful banquet table. Sitting all around were her parents and all the other people she had loved and who had died before her.

They saw her and began calling to her:

"Hello – How are you?"

"We've been waiting for you!"

"Good to see you."

When Saint Peter came by, the woman said to him, "This is such a wonderful place! How do I get in?"

"You have to spell a word," Saint Peter told her.

"Which word?" the woman asked.

"Love."

The woman correctly spelled 'Love', and Saint Peter

welcomed her into Heaven.

About a year later, Saint Peter came to the woman and asked her to watch the Gates of Heaven for him that day.

While the woman was guarding the Gates of Heaven, her husband arrived.

"I'm surprised to see you," the woman said. "How have you been?"

"Oh, I've been doing pretty well since you died," her husband told her.

"I married the beautiful young nurse who took care of you while you were ill.

"And then I won the multi-state lottery.

"I sold the little house you and I lived in and bought a huge mansion.

"And my wife and I travelled all around the world. We were on holiday in Hawaii and I went water skiing today. I fell and hit my head, and here I am. What a bummer! How do I get in?"

"You have to spell a word," the woman told him.

"Which word?" her husband asked.

"Czechoslovakia..."

★

On his death bed a miser said to his wife, "Promise me that when I die you will put all my money in the coffin with me, because I want to have it with me in the afterlife." She did so, and soon after he died.

During the funeral service his wife sat beside her best friend in whom she had confided her promise to her husband.

After the ceremony and just before the undertakers closed the coffin, the wife said, "Wait!" She then placed a box in the coffin. The undertakers locked the casket and they rolled it away.

The friend said, "Myrtle surely you weren't foolish enough to put all your money in there with your husband."

Myrtle replied, "I'm a faithful Catholic, so I cannot go back on my word. I promised him that I was going to do so and I did. I got it all together, put it into my account, and wrote him a cheque....

If he can cash it, then he can spend it."

★

Six people were hanging on a rope, under a helicopter: five men and one woman.

The rope was not strong enough to carry them all, so they decided that one had to leave, because otherwise they were all going to fall.

They weren't able to choose that person, until the woman gave a very touching speech.

She said that she would voluntarily let go of the rope, because, as a woman, she was used to giving up everything for her husband and kids or for men in general, and was used to always making sacrifices with little in return.

As soon as she finished her speech, all the men started clapping...

★

A man is watching the footy on TV when his wife interrupts.

"Darling, would you please fix the dripping tap in the kitchen. It's not working."

He replies impatiently, "Fix the dripping tap? Am I a plumber?"

The wife asks, "Well then would you mow the grass. It looks like a jungle."

To which he says, "Mow the grass? Am I a gardener? Hardly. I don't think so."

"Ok," she says.

"Well would you please wash the car? It's so filthy we can't see out the window."

"I'm not a cleaner and I don't want to wash the car. I'm sick of your nagging. I'm going to the pub."

So he goes to the local pub and watches the footy there with his mates. But when the game's over he feels guilty about his rudeness to his wife.

So he decides to apologise and returns home.

As he opens the front gate, he notices the lawn looking trim. Then notices the car is glistening! When he gets a beer he notices that the kitchen tap is silent.

"Sweety," he asks. "How come the grass is cut, the car is clean and the tap isn't dripping?"

She explains, "After you left I sat on the front verandah and cried. Then a sweet young man asked me what the matter was. I told him and he offered to do all the jobs. In return all he asked for was for me to go to bed with him or to bake him a cake."

The husband said, "So what kind of cake did you bake him?"

She replied, "Bake a cake? Am I a baker?"

★

A police officer pulls over a speeding car. The officer says, "You're 20km over the 100km speed limit."

The male driver replies. "Officer I had it on cruise control at 100, perhaps your radar gun needs checking."

The driver's wife says, "Darling you know that this car doesn't have cruise control."

"Shut up Nancy," snaps the driver as the officer writes a ticket. As he hands the ticket to the driver, he says, "You're not wearing your seat belt. That's a $50 fine," and writes another ticket.

"But officer I took it off when you stopped me, so that I could get my licence from my back pocket."

Nancy says, "Darling, you never wear your seat belt when driving."

The driver is furious and shouts, "Nancy shut up!" as the police officer writes the third ticket.

The officer asks the woman, "Madam does your husband always speak to you like that?"

"Only when he's been drinking."

BEAUTY

A sexually active woman tells her plastic surgeon that she wanted her vaginal lips reduced in size because they were too loose and floppy.

Out of embarrassment she insisted that the surgery be kept a secret and the surgeon agreed.

Awakening from the anaesthesia after the surgery she found three roses carefully placed beside her on the bed.

Outraged, she immediately calls in the doctor. "I thought I asked you not to tell anyone about my operation!"

The surgeon told her he had carried out her wish for confidentiality and that the first rose was from him.

"I felt sad because you went through this all by yourself.

"The second rose is from my nurse. She assisted me in the surgery and empathized because she had the same procedure done some time ago."

"And what about the third rose?" she asked.

"That's from a man upstairs in the burns unit. He wanted to thank you for his new ears."

BIRTHDAYS

Jackie was sick of her old rattletrap car and often complained about it to her husband, Ian. Not long before her birthday, she said:

"Buy me a surprise for my birthday! Something that accelerates from 0 to 100 in 4 seconds! And I'd like a red one!" Happy and excited, Jacky counted down the days to her birthday. Finally, she got the beautiful present Ian had thoughtfully bought her. Red bathroom scales!

Apparently Ian is dead now....

BLONDES

A blonde and her husband are lying in bed listening to the next door neighbour's dog... It has been barking in the backyard for hours and hours. The blonde jumps out of bed and says,

"I've had enough of this," and goes downstairs.

The blonde finally comes back to bed and her husband says, "The dog is still barking, what have you been doing?"

The blonde smiles triumphantly and says,

"I put the dog in our backyard. Let's see how they like it!"

★

Did you hear about the two blondes who froze to death in a drive-in movie? They had gone to see 'Closed for the Winter'.

★

A blonde goes into work one morning crying her eyes out. Her boss asks sympathetically, "What's the matter?" The blonde replies, "Early this morning I got a phone call saying that my mother had passed away."

The boss, feeling sorry for her, says, "Why don't you go home for the day? Take the day off to relax and rest."

"Thanks, but I'd be better off here. I need to keep my mind off it and I have the best chance of doing that here."

The boss agrees and allows the blonde to work as usual.

A couple of hours pass and the boss decides to check on the blonde.

He looks out from his office and sees the blonde crying hysterically.

"What's so bad now? Are you going to be okay?" he asks.

"No!" exclaims the blonde. "I just received a horrible call from my sister. Her mother died, too!"

★

Two blondes are walking down the street.

One notices a compact on the sidewalk and leans down to pick it up.

She opens it, looks in the mirror and says, "Hmm, this person looks familiar."

The second blonde says, "Here, let me see!" So the first blonde hands her the compact.

The second one looks in the mirror and says, "You dummy, it's me!"

★

A plane is on its way to Darwin, when a blonde in economy class stands up and moves to the first class section and sits.

The flight attendant sees her do this and asks to see her ticket.

She then tells the blonde that she paid for economy class so she will have to go back to her old seat.

The blonde replies, "I'm blonde, I'm beautiful, I'm going to Darwin and I'm staying right here."

The flight attendant goes into the cockpit and tells the pilots that there's a blonde bimbo sitting in first class who should be sitting in economy class and refuses to return to her seat.

The co-pilot goes to the blonde and tries to explain that because she only paid for an economy class seat she will have to return to it.

The blonde replies, "I'm blonde, I'm beautiful, I'm going to Darwin and I'm staying right here."

The co-pilot tells the pilot that he probably should radio the police to arrest the blonde when they land. The pilot says, "You say she's blonde? I'll handle this. I'm married to one and I speak blonde."

He goes to the blonde and whispers in her ear. She says "Oh, I'm so sorry," and returns to her seat in economy class.

The flight attendant and co-pilot are astounded and ask him what he said to make her return to her seat.

"I told her that first class isn't going to Darwin."

BOWLS

Eileen and her husband Bob went for counselling after 30 years of marriage.

When asked what the problem was, Eileen went into a passionate, painful tirade listing every problem they had ever had in the 30 years they had been married.

She went on and on and on: neglect, lack of intimacy, emptiness, loneliness, feeling unloved and unlovable, an entire laundry list of unmet needs she had endured over the course of their marriage.

Finally, after allowing this to go on for a sufficient length of time, the therapist got up, walked around the desk and after asking Eileen to stand, embraced her, unbuttoned her blouse and bra, put his hands on her breasts and massaged them thoroughly, while kissing her passionately as her husband Bob watched with a raised eyebrow!

Eileen shut up, buttoned up her blouse, and quietly sat down while basking in the glow of being highly aroused.

The therapist turned to Bob and said, "This is what your wife needs at least three times a week. Can you do this?"

Bob thought for a moment and replied, "Well, I can drop her off here on Mondays and Wednesdays but on Tuesdays, Thursdays and Fridays I play bowls..."

BRAINS

Three rebels face a firing squad in a small Central American country.

The first is placed against the wall and just before the order to shoot him is given, he yells, "Earthquake!"

The firing squad falls into a panic and the rebel jumps over the wall and escapes in the confusion.

The second is placed against the wall. The squad is reassembled and he ponders what his fellow rebel has done.

Before the order to shoot is given, he yells, "Tornado!" Again the squad fall apart and he slips over the wall.

The last person is placed against the wall. He thinks, "I see the pattern here, just scream out a disaster and hop over the wall."

As the firing squad is reassembled and the rifles raised in his direction, he grins and yells, "Fire!"

BRAS

A man walked into the ladies department at Myer and shyly asked the salesgirl to help him select a bra for his wife.

The salesgirl asks him: "What sort of bra?"

"Sort?" the man asks, "There's more than one sort?"

"Oh yes," says the salesgirl, as she points to a vast array of bras in different shapes, sizes, colours and materials.

"But really, there are only four main sorts of bras," she explains to the relieved man who asks what they are.

"There are the Catholic,

the Salvation Army,

the Presbyterian,

and the Baptist bras.

Which one would you prefer?"

Confused and worried, he says that his wife attends the Uniting Church.

"Oh don't worry," she says, "These bras transcend such differences. Let me explain.

"The Catholic type supports the masses;
the Salvation Army type lifts the fallen;
the Presbyterian type keeps them staunch and upright; and
the Baptist type makes mountains out of mole hills."

★

At last all is revealed. Why the letters A, B, C, D, DD, E, F, G, and H are used to define bra sizes.

{A} Almost boobs.

{B} Barely boobs.

{C} Can't Complain boobs

{D} Dangling boobs

{DD} Double Dangling boobs

{E} Enormous boobs

{F} Fake boobs

{G} Get a Reduction... and

{H} the German bra.

Holtzemfromfloppen

BRIGHT SPARKS

My dog was stretched across the back seat and I wanted to impress upon her that she must remain there. I walked to the curb backward, pointing my finger at the car and saying emphatically, "Now you stay. Do you hear me? Stay! Stay!"

The driver of a nearby car, gave me a strange look and said, "Why don't you just put it in 'Park'?"

★

A man boarded the bus with his trouser pockets filled with golf balls and sat next to a school boy. The puzzled school boy kept looking at his bulging pockets. After a while the man noticed and explained, "It's golf balls".

The school boy continued to stare at his pockets. Then not being able to contain his curiosity any longer, he asked, "Does it hurt as much as tennis elbow?"

★

A man is cleaning his rifle and accidentally shoots his wife. He immediately dials 000.

"It's my wife!" he says, "I've accidentally shot her. I think I've killed her?"

Operator: "Please calm down Sir. Can you first make sure she is actually dead?"

...★BANG★ "Okay, I've done that," says the man. "What next?"

★

A bright spark was sent on his way to Heaven. Upon arrival, a concerned St Peter met him at the Pearly Gates.

"I'm sorry," St Peter said. "But Heaven is suffering from an overload of goodly souls and we have been forced to put up an Entrance Exam for new arrivals to ease the burden of Heavenly Arrivals."

"That's cool," said the bright spark. "What does the Entrance Exam consist of?"

"Just three questions," said St Peter.

"Which are?" asked the bright spark.

"The first is:" said St Peter, "which two days of the week start with the letter 'T'?

The second is: how many seconds are there in a year?

The third is: what was the name of the swagman in Waltzing Matilda?"

"Now," said St Peter, "I'll give you a couple of hours to think about these and then I'll ask you for the answers."

So the bright spark gave those three questions much thought.

When time was up St Peter asked, "Which two days of the week start with the letter T?"

The bright spark said, "Today and tomorrow."

St Peter pondered this answer and decided that indeed the answer could be applied to the question.

"Well then, what's your answer to the second question –how many seconds in a year?"

The bright spark replied, "Twelve!"

"Only twelve?" exclaimed St Peter, "How did you arrive at that number?"

"Easy," said the bright spark, "there's the second of January, the second of February, right through to the second of December, giving a total of twelve seconds."

St Peter looked at the bright spark and said, "I need some time to consider your answer before I can give you a decision."

But after a few minutes, St Peter returned to the bright spark and said. "I'll allow the answer to stand, but you need to get the final question absolutely correct to be allowed into Heaven."

"What was the name of the swagman in Waltzing Matilda?"

The bright spark replied, "That's the easiest question. It was Andy of course."

"Really?!"

This flabbergasted St Peter. "How did you arrive at THAT answer?"

"Easy," said the bright spark, "Andy sat, Andy watched, Andy waited 'til his billy boiled."

And lo, the bright spark entered Heaven...

★

Two bright sparks were at the outdoor café when a truck drove past loaded with rolls of turf. "Gosh some people are lucky aren't they?" said Claire as she looked at the disappearing truck.

"What do you mean?" asked Jan. "Fancy having enough money to send your lawn out to be mown," Claire replied.

BRITISH

Did you hear about the Englishman who was stopped by Australian immigration officers at Sydney airport?

They asked him if he had a criminal record.

He replied, "I didn't know it was still necessary."

BUSINESS

A disappointed salesman of a soft drink company was sacked from an assignment to Saudi Arabia.

Back home a friend asked why he was sacked?

The salesman explained, "When I was posted, I was very confident that I'd make a good sales pitch. But I had a problem. I didn't know how to speak Arabic. So I planned to convey the message through three posters. The first poster showed a man lying in the hot desert sand totally exhausted and fainting.

The second poster displayed the man drinking our soft drink.

And the third poster showed our man now totally refreshed.

Then these posters were pasted all over the place."

"That sounds great!" said his friend.

"You'd sure think so. Except for one thing!" said the salesman.

"No one told me they read from right to left!"

CALAMITIES

Several friends met regularly at each other's homes for dinner and then to play cards. When it was Frank and Jenny's turn to host, Jenny decided on a mushroom and chicken pie. Frank suggested she pick the mushrooms in the paddock at the back of their house. Jenny was a bit worried that they might be poisonous. But Frank reminded her that their dog Red ate them and he was okay.

So Jenny decided to give it a try. She picked some and washed, sliced, and diced them for her pie. Then she gave Red some left overs and he wolfed them down. After the meal, which was a great success they settled down to a card game of 500. But a few minutes later the front door bell rang and on Jenny opening the door, the neighbour rushed in crying out, "Red is dead."

Jenny became hysterical. What was going to happen to her guests and Frank and herself? After she finally calmed down, she called the doctor and told him what had happened. The doctor said, "Stay calm. I'll call an ambulance and come as soon as I can. Everything will be fine."

The ambulance soon arrived. The officers and doctor took each person into the bathroom, gave them an enema, and pumped out their stomach.

After they finished, the doctor said, "Everyone should be fine now," and left. They were all feeling weak and slouched on the living room arm chairs when the neighbour whispered to Jenny, "You know, that driver who ran over Red didn't even stop."

CARS

David was telling his wife about his first business trip to London. He had some spare time so took a taxi to get a feel of the city.

After an hour he decided he'd like to stop at a hotel for a drink. He tapped the taxi driver on the shoulder to get his attention.

The driver screeched, lost control of the taxi, nearly hit a car, swerved up a footpath, just missed a pedestrian and stopped inches from a large shop window.

For a few moments there was deathly silence. Then, the driver gasped, "Are you alright? I'm terribly sorry, but you scared the sh... out of me."

David whispered, "I'm so sorry for startling you. I had no idea that a tap on the shoulder would scare you like that."

The driver replied, "No. It was my fault. I'm terribly sorry. Today's my first day driving a taxi. I've been driving a hearse for 10 years."

★

A 60 year old man on a motor scooter pulls up next to a doctor in his sleek car at a street light. The scooter driver looks at the shiny car and asks, "What kind of car ya got there, sonny?"

The doctor replies, "A Bugatti Veyron, and it cost two and half million dollars."

"That's a lot of money," says the scooter driver. "Why's it so pricey?"

"Because it can do up to 267 miles an hour!" says the proud doctor.

The scooter driver asks, "Mind if I peek inside?"

"No problem," replies the doctor.

So the scooter driver pokes his head in the window and looks around. Then, sitting back on his scooter, he says, "That's a pretty nice car, all right, but I'll stick with my scooter!"

Just then the light changes and the doctor decides to show the old man just what his car can do. He floors it, and within 30 seconds the speedometer reads 120 mph.

Suddenly, he notices a dot in his rear view mirror. It seems to be getting closer!

He slows down to see what it could be and whooooooosh!

Something whips by him going much faster!

"What could be going faster than my Bugatti?" the doctor asks himself.

He presses harder on the accelerator and takes the Bugatti up to 150 mph.

Then ahead of him, he sees that it's the old man on the scooter!

Amazed that the scooter could pass his Bugatti, the doctor gives it more petrol and passes the scooter at 200 mph. He's feeling pretty good until he looks in his mirror and sees the old man gaining on him again!

Astounded, the doctor floors the accelerator and takes the Bugatti all the way to 260 mph.

Not ten seconds later, he sees the scooter bearing down on him again! The Bugatti is flat out, and there's nothing he can do!

Suddenly, the scooter ploughs into the back of his Bugatti.

Demolishing the rear end.

The doctor stops and jumps out and amazingly the old man is still alive.

He runs to the smashed up man and says, "I'm a doctor... is there anything I can do for you?"

The old man whispers, "Unhook my braces from your side view mirror."

★

"You know, somebody actually complimented me on my driving today. They left a little note on the windscreen. It said, 'Parking Fine.' So that was nice."

★

After packing the Pope's luggage into the limo, the driver notices the Pope is still standing on the curb.

"Excuse me, Your Holiness," says the driver, "Would you please take your seat so we can leave?"

"Well, I was wondering if you could do me a favour," says the Pope, "they never let me drive at the Vatican when I was a cardinal, and I'd very much like to drive today."

"I'm sorry, Your Holiness, but I cannot let you do that. I'd lose my job! What if something should happen?" protests the driver, wishing he'd never gone to work that morning.

"Who's going to tell?" says the Pope with a smile.

Reluctantly, the driver climbs in the back as the Pope clambers in behind the wheel. The driver quickly regrets his decision when, after exiting the airport, the Pontiff floors it, accelerating the limo to 150 kph.

"Please slow down, Your Holiness!" begs the worried driver, but the Pope keeps the pedal down until they hear sirens.

"Oh, dear God, I'm going to lose my licence - and my job!" moans the driver.

The Pope pulls over and rolls down the window as the policeman approaches, but the policeman takes one look at him, goes back to his motorcycle, and radios headquarters.

"I need to talk to the Police Chief," says the policeman.

The Chief gets on the radio and the policeman tells him that he's stopped a limo going 155 kph.

"So book him," says the Chief.

"I don't think we want to do that, he's really important," says the policeman.

The Chief exclaims, "All the more reason!"

"No, I mean really important," insists the policeman.

The Chief then asks, "Who do you have - the mayor?"

The policeman says, "Bigger."

The chief then asks, "The President?"

The policeman says, "Bigger."

"Well," says the Chief, "who is it?"

The policeman says, "I think it's God!"

The Chief is even more puzzled and curious, "What makes you think it's God?"

The policeman says, "His chauffeur is the Pope!"

CATHOLIC

An altar boy at confession asks, "Please forgive me Father, for I have sinned. I have been with a loose girl."

The priest asks, "Is that you, Carlos Lollita?"

"Yes, Father, it is."

"And who was this loose girl?"

"I can't say Father, because I don't want to ruin her reputation."

"Well, Carlos, I'm sure to find out sooner or later so you may as well tell me now. Was it Maria Marotti?"

"I can't say Father."

"Was it Gina Lorez?"

"Sorry Father, I'll never tell."

"Was it Lucia Fernici?"

"Father, I cannot name her."

"Was it Francesca Briatoi?"

"My lips are sealed."

The priest sighs in frustration. "You're very uncooperative. But I admire the reason why. However you've sinned and have to atone. You cannot be an altar boy now for five months. Now behave yourself."

Carlos walks back to his pew, and his friend Mickelo slides over and whispers, "What'd you get?"

"Five months vacation and four good leads..."

★

A drunkard lurched into a Catholic church and slumped in a confession box without a word.

The priest cleared his throat to encourage the drunk to say something. But the man remained silent. The priest then knocked on the wall twice to get the drunk's attention.

The drunk replied, "Don't bother knockin', mate, there's no paper here either."

★

Patrick, a lapsed Catholic is stricken with guilt and unwillingly feels he had better go to confession so that he can start a new life. He enters the confessional cubicle and is amazed at how things have changed since he was last there. There's a bar with wine, champagne and liqueurs. Beside it is a shelf filled with cigars and chocolates. The door opens and in comes Father O'Farrell.

"Father, please forgive me for not coming to confession all these years," says Patrick. "My, how things have changed. The confessional is so much more inviting than when I was last here," he said.

Father O'Farrell responds: "Get out. This is my side."

★

A married man confessed to his priest, "Please forgive me but I almost had intercourse with another woman."

The priest asked, "What do you mean, almost?"

The married man said, "We went to bed and rubbed each other, but I stopped."

The priest said, "Rubbing together is the same as putting it in. You're not to see that woman again. For your penance, say ten Hail Marys and put $50 in the poor box".

The man said his prayers, and then walked over to the poor box. Took out his money then returned it to his wallet and started to leave.

The priest, who was watching, raced over to him saying, "I saw that. You didn't put any money in the poor box!"

The man replied, "I rubbed the $50 on the box, and according to you, that's the same as putting it in!"

CELIBACY

Benedict, a young monk who is a specialist in ancient texts, has been accepted in a monastery copying such documents.

He joins the other monks copying the church laws by hand.

However, Benedict notices that the monks copy from copies, rather than from the original manuscript.

So, he approaches the head monk and points out that even if a small error was made in the first copy, it might never be found and instead be repeated in all further copies.

The Abbot says, "My son, we have been copying from the copies for centuries, but what you say is right, so I will find the originals."

The Abbot descends into the caves underneath the monastery where the original manuscripts are kept in a vault that has been locked for hundreds of years.

Hours pass and the old Abbot has not re-emerged, missing lunch. Then he is not present at dinner. He misses prayers.

Benedict becomes worried. Surely it wouldn't take this long for the Abbot to find just a few examples, so Benedict goes down to look for him.

He sees the Abbot bent over, weeping and wailing and banging his head with his fists. "We missed the R! We missed the R! We missed the R!" moans the Abbot.

Benedict asks, "What's wrong, Father?"

Choking, the old Abbot can hardly reply, "The word was... 'CELEBRATE'!!!"

CHEATING

One day, at the pub, Bob says to Jack, "The local supermarket has just installed a diagnostic computer. For only $10 you just have to give it a urine sample and the computer will tell you what's wrong and what to do about it. You don't have to pay steep doctor's bills."

As it happened Jack had a sore wrist that kept him awake at nights. So he thought he'd give it a try.

So Jack deposits a urine sample in a small jar and takes it to the supermarket.

He pays $10 and the computer lights up and asks for the urine sample. He pours the sample into the slot and waits.

A few seconds later, the computer spits out a printout:

You have a strained tendon.

Soak your wrist in warm water twice daily, avoid activity and it will improve in two weeks.

After one week his wrist had improved, although it was still sore. He was so impressed with the computer, but he wondered if it could be fooled.

So Jack mixed a stool sample from his cat, urine samples from his wife and son and a sperm sample from himself.

Jack went back to the Supermarket computer, deposited the $10 and poured in the mixture.

A few moments later the computer ejects a paper slip saying:

1. *Your cat has ringworm. Bathe her with anti-fungal shampoo (aisle two).*
2. *Your son is addicted to heroine. Take him to a rehab clinic.*
3. *Your wife is pregnant. Not yours. Find a lawyer.*
4. *Stop playing with yourself, or your wrist will not recover.*

CHILDHOOD ADVENTURES

A woman brings eight year old Tommy home and tells his mother that he was caught playing doctors and nurses with Libby, her eight year old daughter. Tommy's mother says, "Let's not be too hard on them... it's natural to be curious about sex at that age."

"Curious about sex?" replies Libby's mother, "He's taken her appendix out!"

★

Five year old Miriam asked her grandma how old she was.

Grandma replied she was so old, she couldn't remember.

Miriam replied, "If you don't remember, look in the back of your panties. That's what I do. Mine say five to six."

★

"Where did I come from Mummy?' asked seven year old Robert. Mummy had been dreading this question but decided to be truthful. So she explained the sex act and then the pregnancy and then delivery at the local hospital. She watched closely for his reaction.

"I just wondered," said Robert. "The boy who sits beside me at school came from New South Wales."

★

Merle was driving her two young children to granny's one day, when a woman in the convertible ahead stood up and waved. She was completely naked! Merle was shocked. "I can't believe it," she said.

"I can't believe it either," said six year old Shelley.

"Mummy that lady isn't wearing her seat belt!"

★

Four year old Andrew was having a picnic lunch with his parents in a park, when he became fascinated with a young couple kissing on a bench nearby. Without taking his eyes off them, he asked his parents, "Why is he whispering in her mouth?"

★

Two boys, ages 8 and 10, were very mischievous and were always getting into trouble. If any mischief occurred in their town, the two boys were probably involved.

The boys' mother heard that a local minister was good at disciplining children, so she asked him to speak with her boys.

The minister agreed and asked to see them individually. So the mother sent the eight year old in the morning to be followed by the older boy in the afternoon.

The minister, a huge man with a booming voice, sat the younger boy down and asked him sternly, "Do you know where God is, son?"

The boy's mouth dropped open, but he made no response, sitting there wide-eyed with his mouth hanging open.

So the minister repeated the question in an even sterner tone, "Where is God?" Again, the boy made no attempt to answer.

The minister raised his voice even more and shook his finger in the boy's face and bellowed, "Where is God?"

The boy screamed and bolted from the room, ran directly home and dove into his cupboard, slamming the door behind him. When his older brother found him, he asked, "What happened?"

The younger brother, gasping for breath, replied, "We're in BIG trouble this time. GOD is missing, and they think we did it!"

★

A little girl opened the big old family Bible. She was fascinated as she looked through the yellowed pages. Suddenly, something fell out of the book. She picked it up and examined it. It was an old leaf that had been pressed between the pages.

"Mummy, look what I found," the little girl called.

"What is it dear?"

With awe the little girl whispered, "I think it's Adam's underwear!"

★

After the christening of his baby brother in church, Tommy sobbed all the way home in the car. His father asked him three times what was wrong. Finally, the boy replied, "The minister said he wanted us brought up in a Christian home, and I want to stay with you."

★

Police were called to a day care centre where a three year old was resisting a rest.

CHINESE

Hung Chow calls into work and says, "I no come work today, I really sick. Got headache, stomach ache and legs hurt."

The boss says, "Hung Chow, I really need you today. When I feel like this, I go to my wife and tell her to give me sex. That makes everything better and I go to work. You try that."

Two hours later Hung Chow calls again. "I do what you say and I feel great. I be at work soon. You got nice house."

CHURCH

It was Palm Sunday and because of a cold, six year old Tim stayed at home with his dad while his mum and sister Ella went to church. When the family returned they were carrying several palm branches. Tim asked what they were for.

"People placed them on the road for Jesus and his donkey to ride over," Ella said. "Crumbs! The one Sunday I don't go, he shows up!"

★

The Sunday school teacher asked her class on the way to the church service, "And why should you be quiet in church?"

Michelle replied, "Because people are sleeping."

★

During the minister's prayer one Sunday, there was a loud whistle from a back pew. Johnny's mother was horrified. She pinched him into silence and after church asked, "Johnny, why did you do such a thing?"

Johnny answered earnestly, "I asked God to teach me to whistle, and He did!"

CLOCKS

Late one night, after a party Guy invited his friends to see the new city apartment he was renting. Guy, who was a bit tipsy, led the way to his bedroom where a big brass gong was hanging on the wall.

"What's that gong for?" asked one friend.

"Issss nod a gong. Issss a talking clock," Guy replied.

"A talking clock - seriously?"

"Yup." he hiccupped.

"How's it work?" the second friend asked, squinting at it.

"Jus.. watch," Guy said.

He picked up a hammer, gave the gong an ear-shattering bash and stepped back.

His mates stood looking at one another.

Suddenly, a voice from the other side of the wall screamed, "Shut up! You idiot!! It's ten past three in the morning!"

★

Don is on a quiz show. To the surprise of his family and friends he hangs in to the last question.

Quiz Master: "Don this is the million dollar question. Are you ready?"

Don: "Yes."

Quiz Master: "Which of the following birds does not build its own nest? Is it A) robin, B) sparrow, C) cuckoo, or D) thrush?"

Don: "That's simple. It's a cuckoo."

Quiz Master: "Are you sure?"

Don: "I'm sure."

Quiz Master: "You said C) cuckoo, and you're right! Congratulations, you have just won one million dollars!"

To celebrate, Don takes his girlfriend Cheryl to Hawaii. Over dinner she says, "I had no idea you were so clever Don. How did you know it was the cuckoo that didn't build its own nest?"

"That's easy - they live in clocks."

★

A sales representative in Romania was on his way to a meeting and on his way had to go through a village and farm land. However his watch stopped and he was desperate to find out if he could make it to his appointment on time. Spying a man and his donkey resting by the side of the track, he stopped and asked the man if he knew the time. The man turned to his donkey and then held and parted the donkey's balls peering intently. He then said, "12.15pm."

The salesman was amazed thinking he might have hit on a great marketing discovery. "How can you tell the time by separating your donkey's balls?" he asked.

"Easy," said the man, "That way I can see the village clock tower."

COMMUNICATION

On a freezing morning, Melanie emails husband David at work: *"Windows frozen, won't open."*

David emails back, *"Carefully pour some lukewarm water on."*

Shortly after, Melanie texts back:
"Computer now completely stuffed."

★

How women communicate:
1. *Fine:* This is the word women use to end an argument when they are right and you need to shut up.
2. *Five Minutes:* If she is getting dressed, this means half an hour. Five minutes is only five minutes if you have just been given five more minutes to watch the footy before mowing the lawn.
3. *Nothing:* This is the calm before the storm. This means something, and you should be on your toes. Arguments that begin with nothing usually end in *fine*.
4. *Go Ahead:* This is a dare, not permission. Don't Do It!
5. *Loud Sigh:* This is actually a word, but is a non-verbal statement often misunderstood by men. A loud sigh means she thinks you are an idiot and wonders why she is wasting her time standing here and arguing with you about nothing. (Refer back to 3 for the meaning of *nothing*.)
6. *That's Okay:* This is one of the most dangerous statements a women can make to a man. *That's Okay* means she wants to think long and hard before deciding how and when you will pay for your mistake.
7. *Thanks:* A woman is thanking you, do not question, or faint. Just say you're welcome. (I want to add in a clause here - this is true, unless she says *Thanks a lot* - that is PURE sarcasm and she is not thanking you at all. DO NOT say *you're welcome*. That will bring on a *whatever*).

8. *Whatever:* Is a woman's way of saying *Go to Hell*.

9. *Don't worry about it, I got it:* Another dangerous statement, meaning this is something that a woman has told a man to do several times, but is now doing it herself. This will later result in a man asking *What's wrong?* For the woman's response refer to 3.

★

Travelling on the Princes Highway and needing to use the toilet, I stopped at a rest area and headed to the toilet.

I'd hardly sat down when I heard a voice from the next cubicle saying, "Hi, how are you?"

I'm not the type to start a conversation in the toilet and I don't know what got into me, But I answered, somewhat embarrassed, "I'm fine!"

And the other person says, "So what are you up to?"

What kind of question is that? At that point, I'm thinking this is too bizarre so I say, "Uhhh, I'm like you, just traveling!"

Now I'm trying to get out as fast as I can when I hear another question. "Can I come over?"

Ok, this question is just too weird for me but I thought I'd be polite and end the conversation, so I say, "No..I'm a little busy right now!!!"

Then I hear the person say nervously, "Listen, I'll have to call you back. There's an idiot in the other cubicle who keeps answering all my questions."

COMPUTERS

Dear Tech Support,

Last year I upgraded from Boyfriend to Husband and noticed a slowdown in system performance, particularly in the flower and jewellery applications, which operated flawlessly under Boyfriend.

Also, Husband uninstalled many other valuable programmes, such as Romance and Personal Attention and then installed undesirable programs such as: Football, Cricket and Going to the Pub with Mates. Conversation no longer runs, and Housecleaning simply crashes the system. I've tried running Nagging to fix these problems, but with no success.

What can I do?

Signed, Desperate

Dear Desperate,

First keep in mind, Boyfriend is an Entertainment Package, while Husband is an Operating System. Please enter the command: 'http: I Thought You Loved Me.html' and try to download Tears.

Don't forget to install the Guilt update. If that application works as designed, Husband should then automatically run the applications Jewellery and Flowers, but remember – overuse of the above application can cause Husband to default to Grumpy Silence, Garden Shed or Beer. Beer is a very bad program that will download the Snoring Loudly.

Whatever you do, DO NOT install Mother-in-law (it runs a virus in the background that will eventually seize control of all your system resources). Also, do not attempt to reinstall the

Boyfriend program. These are unsupported applications and will crash Husband.

In summary, Husband is a great system, but it does have limited memory and cannot learn new applications quickly. It also tends to work better running one task at a time. You might consider buying additional software to improve memory and performance. We recommend Food and Hot Lingerie.

Good Luck,

Tech Support

CRIME

A man was on trial for murder. There was strong evidence suggesting he was guilty, but no corpse had been found.

The defence lawyer knowing that his client would probably be found guilty decided to use a trick.

"Ladies and gentlemen of the jury, I have a surprise for you all," the lawyer said. "In one minute, the person presumed dead in this case will walk into this courtroom." He looked toward the courtroom door. As did all the amazed jurors.

The lawyer checked his watch. A minute had passed. But no one had entered the court room.

At last, the lawyer said, "Members of the jury I invented the previous statement. No corpse has been found. But you all looked at the door eagerly waiting to see the person presumed dead enter. It is clear that you have a reasonable doubt as to whether anyone was killed, and therefore, you must in all honesty return a verdict of not guilty."

The jury retired to decide on their verdict. Soon after they returned and pronounced the accused guilty.

"How can you justify this?" asked the lawyer. "It was clear that you had some doubt or you would not have stared at the door."

The jury foreman responded, "That's true, we looked but the accused didn't!"

★

Carlos, an elderly Italian who lived alone, wanted to plant his annual vegie garden, but it was too difficult for him as the ground was hard. His only son Frederico, who used to dig his garden was in jail. In his weekly letter to his son, Carlos wrote:

Dear Frederico,

I misse you and ame sad, because I might note be able to have my usual vege garden this year. I am feeling too olde to be digging upe the ground anymore. I knowe that if you were here you woulde helpe me oute and dig it upe for me.

Love,

Papa

A week later Frederico's response arrived.

Dear Papa,

Don't dig up your garden. That's where the body is buried.

Love,

Rico

At 2 a.m. the next morning, police arrived and dug up the entire garden without finding the body. They apologized to the old man and left.

That same day Carlos received another letter from Frederico.

Dear Papa,
   You can plant the vegie garden now. That's the best I could do.
   Love,
   Rico

CULTURAL TRADITIONS

A Somalian man is given permission to live in Australia. Jabril rents and moves into a small house near Mildura, Victoria. A few days later Kev, the friendly next door neighbour, decides to visit and welcome him.

But walking up the drive he sees the Somalian running around his front yard in circles chasing several hens. Not wanting to interrupt these Somalian practises, Kev decides to welcome him the next day.

The next morning Kev tries again, but just before he knocks on the front door, he sees through the window the Somalian man urinating into a glass and then drinking it!

"Blimey what a strange custom," he thought. He wanted to be culturally sensitive so decided to welcome his neighbour another day.

The third day he tries again. But 'lo and behold!' he sees his new neighbour leading a bull down the driveway and then put his head next to the bull's bum.

Kev can't take any more and marches up to his neighbour and says, "Hey Mate, what is it with your customs? I come to welcome you to the neighbourhood, and see you running around in circles after hens. Then the next day you're pissing in a glass – and drinking it! Now you had your head so close to that bull's bum, it could shit on you."

The Somalian (who learnt English while he was in the Detention Centre) is amazed and says, "Sorry sir, you not understand, these are not Somalian ways. I doing Australian customs."

"What do you mean mate?" asks Kev. "Those aren't Aussie ways."

"Yes they are. Back home I learnt on TV," replied Jabril. "Man say to become true Australian, I learn chase chicks, drink piss, and listen to bullshit."

DANGER

A surgeon and a philosopher were on safari when they were ambushed by a tiger, a hippopotamus and a lion. The philosopher who was holding their one rifle with only two bullets left, dithered. So the surgeon grabbed the rifle, shot the philosopher with the two bullets and made a quick getaway.

DARK HUMOUR

Fred was sitting at the bar staring at his drink when a large, aggressive bikie grabbed his drink and swigged it down...

He stared at Fred with his hands on his hips and said, "Well, whatcha' gonna do about it?"

Then Fred burst into tears.

"Hey Man," the bikie said, "Wacha doin'? I can't stand seein' a man cryin'."

"This is the worst day of my life," Fred said. "I'm a total failure. My boss fired me. Then my car was stolen from the work car park and I don't have any insurance. I left my wallet in the taxi I took home. There I found my wife in bed with my best friend and then my dog bit me.

"So I came here to get the courage to end it all. I buy a drink, I drop a tablet in it and watch the poison dissolve; then you show up and drink the whole thing! But enough about me, how're you going?"

★

Fear swept a city hospital's intensive care unit as patients always died in the same bed every Monday at 10 a.m. regardless of their medical problem. This concerned the doctors, some thinking it might have a supernatural cause. Word spread about this phenomenon. Experts from around the world gathered on a Monday to try and find the cause. Shortly before 10 a.m. they assembled some holding crosses and Bibles to protect them from Satan. At the stroke of 10 a.m. in came the part-time cleaner, Doug Thompson. He made straight for the bed, unplugged the life support system, and plugged in the vacuum cleaner...

★

The cost of rehabilitating two seals after a massive oil spill off Canada was $15,000. A cheering crowd assembled to witness the two healthy seals being released back into the wild.

A few minutes later the onlookers saw a giant shark eat them both.

DEATH

One evening three old friends were discussing what they would like family and friends to say about them when viewing them at their funeral.

Robert said, "I would like them to say I was a wonderful husband, a great family man and a faithful friend."

Arthur said, "I would like them to say I was a wonderful teacher and was always ready to help people."

Bert said, "I'd like them to say: 'Look, he's moving!'"

★

An elderly man lay dying in his bed. While suffering the agonies of impending death, he suddenly smelled the aroma of his favourite fruit scones wafting up the stairs.

He gathered his remaining strength, and lifted himself from the bed. Leaning on the wall, he slowly made his way out of the bedroom, and with even greater effort, gripping the railing with both hands, he crawled downstairs.

With laboured breath, he leaned against the door-frame, gazing into the kitchen. Were it not for death's agony, he would have thought himself already in heaven, for there, spread out upon the kitchen table were literally hundreds of his favourite fruit scones.

Was it heaven? Or was it one final act of love from his devoted wife of sixty years, seeing to it that he left this world a happy man?

Mustering one great final effort, he threw himself towards the table, landing on his knees in rumpled posture. His aged and withered hand trembled towards a scone at the edge of the table, when it was suddenly smacked by his wife with a wooden spoon.

"Get off!" she shouted, "they're for the funeral."

★

A man who's just died is delivered to the mortuary wearing an expensive, expertly tailored grey suit. The mortician asks the widow how she would like the body dressed. He points out that the man looks good in the grey suit he's wearing.

The widow however, says that she always thought her husband looked his best in blue and that she wants him in a blue suit.

She gives the mortician a blank cheque and says, "I don't care what it costs, but please have my husband in a blue suit for the viewing."

The widow returns the next day for the wake.

To her delight, she finds her husband dressed in a gorgeous blue suit with a subtle chalk stripe; the suit fits him perfectly.

She says to the mortician, "Whatever this cost, I'm very satisfied. You did an excellent job and I'm very grateful. How much did you spend?"

To her astonishment, the mortician returns the blank cheque.

"There's no charge," he says.

"No really, I must compensate you for the cost of that exquisite blue suit," she says.

"Honestly madam," the mortician says, "it cost nothing. You see, a deceased man of about your husband's size was brought in shortly after you left yesterday and he was wearing an attractive blue suit.

"I asked his wife if she minded him going to his grave wearing a grey suit instead and she said it made no difference as long as he looked nice.

"So I just switched the heads."

★

Doug Smith is on his deathbed, knowing the end is near. His nurse, his wife, his daughter and two sons are with him. So, he says to them,

"Bernie, I want you to take the Toorak houses. Sybil, take the apartments over in South Yarra. Jamie, I want you to take the offices over in the city centre. Sarah, my dear wife, please take all the residential buildings in Carlton."

The nurse is just blown away by all this, and as Doug slips away, she says,

"Mrs. Smith, your husband must have been such a hard-working man to have accumulated all that property."

Sarah replies, "Property? No such luck! He had a paper round!"

DISCRIMINATION

A young ventriloquist is performing at the Melbourne Comedy Festival and with his puppet he goes through his usual repertoire of dumb blonde jokes. Suddenly, a blonde woman in the front row stands and shouts, "Stop those insulting, stupid blonde jokes. How dare you stereotype blonde women that way! Hair colour has nothing to do with a person's intelligence. It's men like you who strip women like me of respect. This attitude is like a cancer that prevents us from full equality at work and positions of honour. You're not only discriminating against blondes but against women in general."

The chastened ventriloquist hastens to apologise, but the blonde interrupts him and yells, "It's not you I'm talking to but that dwarf on your lap."

DRINK

A couple are awakened at 2 a.m. by a loud knocking on the front door.

Mike gets out of bed and goes to the door where a drunken stranger, standing in the pouring rain, asks for a push.

"No, it's 2 a.m.," says Mike. He slams the door and returns to bed.

"Who was that?" asks his wife, Jan.

"Oh a drunk asking for a push," he answers.

"Did you help him?" she asks.

"No, I did not. It's 2 a.m. in the morning and it's pouring rain out there!"

"Well, you have a short memory," says Jan. "Can't you remember last year when we broke down, and that man helped us? I think you should help him, and you should be ashamed of yourself! God loves drunk people too you know."

Mike does as he is told, gets dressed, and goes out into the pounding rain.

He calls out into the dark, "Hello, are you still there?"

"Yes," comes the answer.

"Do you still need a push?" calls out Mike.

"Yes, please!" comes the reply from the dark.

"Where are you?" Mike asks.

"Over here on the swing," replies the drunk.

★

A man around 40 is running along the main street at around 4 a.m. He is stopped by a policeman who asks him what he's doing up at this time of night.

The man replies, "I'm on my way to a lecture about gambling, alcohol abuse and staying out late."

The policeman asks, "Who'd give such a lecture at this time?"

"My wife," the man replies.

★

A wine shop's regular taster moved to France to improve his skills. The owner advertised the position. Months passed but he couldn't find anyone with the necessary expertise.

One day a drunk in dirty clothes arrives for an interview. The owner wonders how he could get rid of him. He gives him a glass to taste.

The drunk sips the wine and correctly recognizes that the drink is a cabernet two years old, grown on a southern slope, matured in steel containers, of ordinary grade, but adequate.

'Obviously this drunk knows something,' thinks the owner. So he tests him on another wine.

"This is a Sauvignon Blanc, six years of age, grown on a north western slope, matured in oak barrels and requires four more years for best results."

'Hmm,' thinks the owner, 'It's not going to be so easy to get rid of him.'

He gives the drunk another glass to try. Again, he's spot on.

"This is a pinot noir and a rare fine grade," he says.

The owner is impressed, but he still doesn't want to employ this man. So he thinks of a test that the drunk would be sure to fail.

He whispers to his red-haired secretary, who promptly leaves the room and soon returns with a glass of urine.

The drunk tries it and spits it out. "It's a 20 year old red-head, four months pregnant - and if I don't get this job, I'll name the father."

★

Aircraft mechanics Cazza and Bazza were mates who'd worked together for years at Hobart Airport.

One day a particularly heavy fog closed the airport and the mates had nothing to do. They were so bored that Cazza said, "Hey Baz, I wish we could have a drink."

"Me too," said Bazza. "Hey we could try some jet fuel. I hear it gives you a real high."

"Great. Let's give it a go."

The mates poured some jet fuel in their mugs and found it a good drop. Before long they were as drunk as skunks.

The next day Cazza woke up with no hangover. Fantastic!

Then his 'phone rang. "Caz. How'ya goin'?" asked Bazza.

"Great!" said Cazza. "I don't have a hangover. How're you goin'?"

"Good as gold," said Bazza.

"Good one! Let's do it again," said Cazza.

"Er, there's just one thing," said Bazza.

"What?"

"Have you farted yet?"

"No."

"Well I have. And I'm in Darwin!"

★

Last night I was out with me mates and had way too much beer. Knowing I was drunk, I did something I'd never done before. I took a bus home. I arrived home safely and I was really pleased, 'cause I'd never driven a bus before!

DRIVING

A woman was making a breakfast of fried eggs for her husband. Suddenly, her husband burst into the kitchen. "Careful," he said, "careful! Put in some more butter! Oh my gosh! You're cooking too many at once. Too many! Turn them! Turn them now! We need more butter. Oh my gosh! Where are we going to get more butter? They're going to stick! Careful. Careful! I said be careful! You never listen to me when you're cooking! Never! Hurry up! Are you crazy? Have you lost your mind? Don't forget to salt them. You know you always forget to salt them. Use the salt! Use the salt! The salt!"

The wife stared at him. "What in the world is wrong with you? You think I don't know how to fry a couple of eggs?"

The husband calmly replied, "I just wanted to show you what it feels like when I'm driving."

★

Franz is the Pastor of the local Lutheran Church and Pastor Konrad is his assistant. One day they pound a sign into the ground, which reads:

Da end iz near!

Turn yourzelf arount now

Before it iz too late!

As a car speeds past, the driver leans out his window and yells, "Stop your doomsdaying you German religious nuts!"

The car disappears around the bend in the road, then a few moments later they hear screeching tyres and a big splash.

Shaking his head, Pastor Franz says, "Dat is ze zird one diz morning."

"Yaa," Pastor Konrad agrees. "Do you zink maybe de zign

should just say, 'Bridge Down'?"

★

Manfred was driving home one evening when a traffic camera flashed. He thought it strange because he wasn't exceeding the speed limit. So to check he was right, he did a u turn and went through the same place making sure that he was driving within the limit. But the camera flashed again. This was weird he thought, so he did another u turn and went even slower through the same spot again, and sure enough, the camera flashed yet again. What a joke! He repeated the exercise a fourth time, this time laughing out loud as the camera flashed. He and his wife had a chuckle about it that evening.

A few weeks later, he got four traffic fines – for driving without his head lights.

★

This morning on the freeway, I looked to my left and saw a woman in a brand new Rolls doing 100 kph with her face up close to her rear view mirror putting on eyeliner.

I looked away for a couple of seconds and when I looked back, unbelievably she was halfway in my lane, still working on that makeup!

I don't scare easily. But she scared me so much that I dropped my electric shaver which knocked the donut out of my other hand! In all the confusion of trying to straighten the car using my knees against the steering wheel, it knocked my cell phone away from my ear which fell into the coffee between my legs, ruining the phone and soaking my trousers. Damn women drivers!

EMBARRASSMENT

A couple, Phil and Carol, drove to the shopping centre, where their car broke down in the car park.

Phil told Carol to do the shopping while he fixed the car. Carol returned later to see several people standing round the car. As she came closer she saw a pair of hairy legs sticking out from under the car.

Unfortunately the lack of underpants revealed normally private parts hanging out the side of his shorts.

Carol quickly stepped forward, put her hand up his shorts, and tucked everything back into place.

On regaining her feet, she looked across the bonnet and found herself staring at her husband, who was standing by watching.

The mechanic however, had to have six stitches in his forehead.

EMERGENCY

I still don't know why I failed a Health and Safety course at work today. One of the questions was: "In case of fire, what steps would you take?"

"Huge ones" was apparently the wrong answer.

ENVIRONMENT

Bert proudly takes his mate Geoff to his backyard to show how environmentally friendly he is. "We grow all our fruit and vegies. I put up that rainwater tank and we use it for all our needs. Then those solar panels give us all the electricity we need. There's Gertie our chook, who supplies us with eggs, and when she stops laying we'll eat her."

Then the friends go inside to watch the footy on Bert's recycled television set.

Meanwhile, Gertie sneaks off to the corner store where the storekeeper Egbert greets her like an old friend. "Hi Gert, you've come for another dozen eggs have you?"

★

No trees were killed in the sending of this message.

However, a large number of electrons were terribly inconvenienced.

★

Last year I replaced all the windows in my house with that expensive double-pane energy efficient kind, and today, I got a call from the contractor who installed them.

He complained that he'd finished the work a year ago and I still hadn't paid him. Really! Does he think I'm stupid? So, I told him just what his fast talking salesman had told me, that in one year these windows would pay for themselves!

"For goodness sake! It's been a year." I told him!

There was silence at the other end of the line, so I finally hung up. He never called back.

★

All those doomsdayers about Climate Change are bad sports. They're not talking about the opportunities Climate Change will bring. As the planet heats up there's going to be some cool new jobs. For instance: Swimming Instructors, Gondola Operators, Stilts Manufacturers, Bleached Coral Hand-painters, Political Bodyguards, Political Hitmen, Insurance Assessors, Border Security Guards, People Smugglers and Raindance Choreographers.

★

Tips from *Green and Proud Of It* by Eartha Waters.

A. In winter wear an extra layer of clothing and put your heater down to 21 degrees, so that you don't use too much energy to warm yourself, particularly with that nasty coal.

I thought being green and proud of it, I'd put my heater down to 10 degrees and put on ten layers of clothing instead. I don't mind looking cuddly.

B. Check your ecological footprint.

Go onto the Internet and work out your ecological footprint. How much impact you're making on the planet, with what you buy, trips you make, water and energy you use and that sort of thing.

I was shocked. If everyone lived like I used to live, we would need about seven planets. I thought – I know what I'll do. I'm going to make my footprint smaller. So I bunch up my toes and wear smaller shoes now. It does pinch a bit and I can't walk too far but it's worth it.

C. Eat less red meat.

So I thought that's it. No more red meat for me. I went to the butcher to see if there were any other kinds of meat I could eat. And there were. They were all pink!

D. If it blinks, switch it off!

Now that is hard because I have a dear friend Violet, who blinks all the time. When she visits, how can I tell her to switch it off?

E. Short efficient showers.

My shower is quite tall. I mean it reaches up to the ceiling. So it can't be efficient. I have asked my hubby to put in a false ceiling, so that the shower can become short and efficient. So he's added that to his long list of things to do.

F. Buy less.

When you buy less you use less energy or water or forests and so on. And you also save money.

So I use my friends' things. But it's very strange. My friends don't seem to like it. They grumble about this. They're not very green are they?

G. Look for the stars.

Well I went outside every night and looked for the stars. My hubby got angry because I was spending all my evenings outside. Then he explained to me that 'look for the stars' means when you buy whitegoods you have to get those with the most stars, because they use less energy and water.

H. Be political to make big changes.

So I'm going to see our Prime Minister right now and show him how to be green and proud of it.

EXERCISE

If you're going to try cross-country skiing, start with a small country.

★

I was totally out of shape, so I enrolled in an aerobics class for seniors. I bent, twisted, gyrated, jumped up and down, and perspired for an hour. But, by the time I got my leotards on, the class was over.

★

Dear Diary,

For my birthday this year, my dear daughter bought me a week of personal training at the local health centre. I booked the training with a personal trainer named David. The club encouraged me to keep a Diary to chart my progress.

Monday: Started my day at 6:00 a.m. Tough to get out of bed, but found it was well worth it when I arrived at the health club to find David waiting for me. He's like a Greek god - with blonde hair, dancing eyes and a dazzling white smile. Wow! David was encouraging as I did my sit-ups, although my gut ached from holding it in while he was around. This is going to be a great week!

Tuesday: I drank a pot of coffee and finally made it out the door.
David made me lie on my back and push a heavy iron bar into the air then he put weights on it! My legs were a little wobbly on the treadmill, but I made the full mile. David's rewarding smile made it all worthwhile. I feel great!

Wednesday: The only way I can brush my teeth is by laying the toothbrush on the counter and moving my mouth back and forth over it. I believe I have a hernia in both pectorals. Driving was okay as long as I didn't try to steer or stop.

David was impatient with me, insisting that my screams bothered other club members. His voice is a little too perky for early in the morning and when he scolds he gets this nasally whine that is VERY annoying. My chest hurt when I got on the treadmill, so David put me on the stair monster. Why the hell would anyone invent a machine to simulate an activity rendered obsolete by elevators? David told me it would help me get in shape and enjoy life.

Thursday: David was waiting for me with his vampire-like teeth exposed as his thin, cruel lips were pulled back in a full snarl. I couldn't help being half an hour late. It took me that long to tie my shoes. David took me to work out with dumbbells. When he wasn't looking, I ran and hid in the toilet. He sent some skinny bitch to find me. Then as punishment he put me on the rowing machine – which I sank.

Friday: I hate that David more than any human being has ever hated any other human being in the history of the world. Stupid, anaemic, anorexic creep. If there was a part of my body I could move without unbearable pain, I would beat him with it. David wanted me to work on my triceps. I don't have any triceps! And if you don't want dents in the floor, don't hand me the damn barbells or anything that weighs more than a sandwich. The treadmill flung me off and I landed on a health and nutrition teacher.

Why couldn't it have been someone softer, like the drama coach or the choir director?

Saturday: David left a message on my answering machine in his grating, shrilly voice wondering why I did not show up today. Just hearing him made me want to smash the machine with my planner. However, I lacked the strength to even use the TV remote and ended up catching eleven straight hours of the Weather Channel.

Sunday: I've asked the Church van to pick me up for services today so that I can thank God that this week is over. I will also pray that next year my daughter will choose a gift for me that is fun -- like a root canal or a hysterectomy. I still say if God had wanted me to bend over, he would have sprinkled the floor with diamonds.

★

Exercise for people over 40. Start by standing on a comfortable surface, where you have plenty of room on each side.

With a 1 kilo potato bag in each hand, extend your arms straight out from your sides and hold them there as long as you can. Try to reach a full minute, and then relax.

Each day you'll find that you can hold this position for just a bit longer.

After a couple of weeks, move up to 5 kilo potato bags.

Then try 25 kilo potato bags and then eventually, try to lift a 50 kilo potato bag in each hand and hold your arms straight for more than a full minute.

...After you feel confident at that level, put a potato in each bag.

★

A. Walking can add minutes to your life, this enables you at 85 years old to spend an additional 5 months in a nursing home at $4,000 a month.

B. My grandfather started walking three km a day at 65. Now he's 80 and we don't know where the hell he is.

C. My friend told me the only reason she took up exercise was to hear heavy breathing again.

D. I joined a gym a year ago for $500 and haven't lost an ounce. Apparently you have to attend the gym.

E. I like long walks, especially when they're taken by people who annoy me.

F. I have flabby thighs, but fortunately my stomach covers them.

G. Every time I hear the dirty word 'exercise', I wash my mouth out with chocolate.

FAIRY TALES

What really happened that fateful morning...

Baby Bear sits in his chair at the table, looks into his small empty bowl. And whines, "Who's been eating my porridge?"

Daddy Bear sits in his chair, looks into his empty large bowl and roars, "Who's been eating my porridge?"

Mummy Bear puts her head through the servery from the kitchen and shouts, "For goodness sake, how many times do I have to go through this with you twits?

"It was Mummy Bear who got up first. It was Mummy Bear who woke everyone in the house. It was Mummy Bear who made the coffee. It was Mummy Bear who unloaded the dishwasher from last night and put everything away. It was Mummy Bear who swept the floor in the kitchen. It was Mummy Bear who went out in the cold early morning air to fetch the newspaper and croissants. It was Mummy Bear who set the damn table. It was Mummy Bear who walked the dog, cleaned the cat's litter tray, gave them their food, and refilled their water.

"And now that you've decided to drag yourselves to the table with your grumpy presence, listen carefully, because I'm only going to say this once.... **I haven't made the porridge yet!**"

★

Once during the holidays, Janice took her four year old daughter Kate, with her to deliver Meals on Wheels to the elderly. Kate was intrigued by various appliances like canes, walkers and wheelchairs. But when she saw false teeth soaking in a glass she was fascinated. She observed in a loud voice, "The tooth fairy will never believe this!"

★

Once upon a time in a land far far away a beautiful, educated, confident princess spied a frog as she sat contemplating the meaning of the universe by a pond in the castle garden. The frog hopped into the princess's lap and said, "Beautiful princess, I was once a handsome young prince, until an evil witch cast a spell on me. One kiss from you, however, and I will be restored to my former glory. Then we could marry and live in your castle with my mother, and you could cook my meals, clean my clothes, bear my children and forever be grateful and happy doing so."

That night the princess dined sumptuously – on white wine and onion cream sauce over lightly sautéed frog legs.

FAMILIES

Families are like fudge... mostly sweet with a few nuts.

★

A man is on the operating table before surgery by a renowned surgeon, who is also his son. Before he receives the anaesthetic, he insists on speaking to his son, the surgeon.

"Yes, dad, what is it?"

"Don't be nervous, son. Do your best, and remember, if it doesn't go well, if something happens to me, your mother is going to come and live with you and your wife..."

★

FARMERS

A Northern Territory jackeroo is overseeing his herd when suddenly a brand-new red BMW emerges out of a dust cloud and screams to a stop. The driver, a young man in a designer suit and sunglasses, leans out the window and says to the jackeroo, "If I tell you how many sheep you have, will you give me a lamb?"

The jackeroo looks at the man, obviously a yuppie, then looks at his peacefully grazing herd and calmly answers, "Sure, why not?"

The yuppie parks his car, whips out his notebook computer, connects it to his mobile phone, and surfs the Internet, where he calls up a GPS satellite to get the exact fix on his location which he then feeds to another satellite that scans the area in an ultra-high-resolution photo.

The young man then opens the digital photo and exports it to an image processing facility. In seconds, he receives an email that the image has been processed and the data stored. He then accesses database through a spreadsheet with email on his smart phone and, after a few minutes, receives a response.

Finally, he prints out a full-color, 150-page report on his hi-tech, miniaturised LaserJet printer, turns to the farmer and says, "You have exactly 1,586 sheep and lambs."

"That's right. Well, I guess you can take one of my lambs," says the Jackaroo.

He watches the young man select one of the animals and looks on bemused as the young man stuffs it into the trunk of his car.

Then the Jackaroo says to the young man, "Hey, if I can tell you exactly what your business is, will you give me back my lamb?"

The young man thinks about it for a second and then says, "Okay, why not?"

"You work for the Australian Government," says the Jackeroo.

"Wow! That's correct," says the yuppie, "but how did you guess that?"

"No guessing required," answered the Jackeroo. "You showed up here even though nobody called you; you want to get paid for an answer I already knew, to a question I never asked. You used all kinds of expensive equipment that clearly somebody else has paid for. You tried to show me how much smarter than me you are; and you don't know a thing about sheep. This is a herd of cattle. Now give me back my dog."

★

A man owned a small farm in Charlton, Victoria. The Farm Workers' Union claimed he was not paying proper wages to his staff and sent a representative to interview him. "I need a list of your employees and how much you pay them," demanded the union rep.

"Well," replied the farmer, "there's my farm hand who's been with me for three years. I pay him $200 a week plus free room and board. The cook/housekeeper has been here for 18 months, and I pay her $150 per week plus free room and board. Then there's the half-wit. He works about 18 hours every day and does about ninety percent of all the work around here. He makes about $20 a week, pays his own room and board, and I buy him a bottle of beer every Saturday night. He also sleeps with my wife occasionally."

"That's the guy I want to talk to... the half-wit," says the union rep agent.

"That would be me," replied the farmer.

★

Farmer John lived on a quiet rural highway west of Geelong. As time went by, the traffic increased in the area. The traffic got so heavy and so fast that Farmer John's free range chickens were being run over at a rate of three to six a day. So John called the local policeman to complain.

"You've got to do something about all these people driving so fast and killing my chickens."

"What do you want me to do?" asked the policeman.

"I don't care. Just do something about those crazy drivers!"

So the next day the policeman asked the council to put up a sign that said: SLOW: SCHOOL CROSSING.

Three days later Farmer John called the policeman and

said, "You've still got to do something about these drivers. The school crossing sign doesn't make any difference!"

So this time, the policeman asked the council to put up a new sign: SLOW: CHILDREN AT PLAY. That didn't make any difference either. So Farmer John called and called every day for three weeks. Finally, he said to the policeman "Your signs are no good. Can I put up my own?"

'Anything to get him off my back', thought the policeman, so he agreed.

He then got no more calls from Farmer John.

Three weeks later, curiosity got the better of the policeman so he gave Farmer John a call.

"How's the problem with those drivers. Did you put up your sign?"

"I sure did," replied Farmer John, "and not one chicken has been killed since then. I've got to go. I'm very busy."

The policeman was really curious now and decided to see the sign for himself. Perhaps it might be something the police could use to slow down traffic elsewhere.

So he drove to John's farm and his jaw dropped the moment he saw the sign. It was spray painted on a sheet of plywood...
NUDIST COLONY
Slowdown and watch out for chicks!

★

A big city lawyer went duck hunting in rural Queensland. He shot a bird, but it fell into a farmer's field on the other side of a fence.

As the lawyer climbed over the fence, an elderly farmer drove up on his tractor and asked him what he was doing.

The lawyer responded, "I shot a duck and it fell in this field, and I'm going to retrieve it."

The old farmer replied, "This is my property, and you're not coming over here."

The indignant lawyer said, "Look I'm one of the best trial lawyers in Australia and, if you don't let me get that duck, I'll sue you and take everything you own."

The old farmer smiled and said, "Apparently, you don't know how disputes are resolved in the outback. We settle small disagreements like this with the 'Three Kick Rule.'"

The lawyer asked, "What's the 'Three Kick Rule'?"

The farmer replied, "Well, because the dispute occurs on my land, I go first. I kick you three times and then you kick me three times and so on, back and forth until someone gives up."

The lawyer quickly thought about the proposed contest and decided that he could easily take on the old codger. He agreed to abide by the local custom.

The old farmer slowly climbed down from the tractor and walked up to the barrister. His first kick planted the tip of his heavy steel toed work boot into the lawyer's groin and dropped him to his knees!

His second kick to the midriff sent the lawyer's last meal gushing from his mouth. The lawyer was on all fours when the farmer's third kick to his rear end, sent him face-first into a fresh cowpat.

Summoning every bit of his will and remaining strength the lawyer very slowly managed to get to his feet. Wiping his face with the arm of his jacket, he said, "Okay, you old fart. Now it's my turn."

The old farmer smiled and said, "Nah, I give up. You can have the duck."

FEISTY WOMEN

A very attractive woman goes up to a bar in a quiet rural pub. She gestures alluringly to the bartender who comes over immediately. When he arrives, she seductively signals that he should bring his face closer to hers. When he does she begins to gently caress his full beard. "Are you the manager?" she murmurs, softly stroking his face with both hands.

"Er, no," the man replies.

"Can you get him for me? I need to speak to him," she says, running her hands beyond his beard and into his hair.

"I'm afraid I can't," breathes the bartender. "Is there anything I can do?"

"Yes, there is. I need you to give him a message," she continues, running her forefinger across the bartender's lips and slyly popping a couple of her fingers into his mouth and allowing him to suck them gently.

"What should I tell him?" the bartender manages to say.

"Tell him," she whispers, "there is no toilet paper, hand soap, or paper towel in the ladies room."

★

Barry was going to marry Sandra, so his father sat him down for a man to man talk. "Barry let me give you the secret to the success of my marriage with your mother. On my wedding night I took off my pants, handed them to your mother, and said, 'Here - try these on.' She did and said, 'These are too big, I can't wear them.' I replied, 'Exactly, I wear the pants in this family and I always will.' Ever since that night we never had any problems."

"Hmmm," said Barry. He thought that might be worth

trying. On his honeymoon, Barry took off his pants and said to Sandra, "Here – try these on."

She tried them on and said, "These are too large. They don't fit me."

Barry said, "Exactly. I wear the pants in this family and I always will. I don't want you to ever forget that."

Then Sandra took off her pants and handed them to Barry. She said, "Here – you try on mine."

He did and said, "I can't get into your pants."

Sandra said, "Exactly. And if you don't change your attitude, you never will."

FESTIVITIES

Three mates were enjoying a Christmas Eve drink together at the local pub. It was around 10 p.m. when one of them remembered that a friend of his was holding a party down the road and had invited him and any of his friends to attend. When they arrived, the host said, "You have to show something that symbolises Christmas."

Jake rummaged in his pockets and pulled out his bunch of keys. "They're bells," he said.

"Good one," said the host.

Bert took out a box of matches. He lit one and said, "It's a candle."

"Fine," said the host.

Frank rummaged in his back pockets and pulled out a panty.

"What's that supposed to symbolise?" asked the host.

"They're Carol's," Frank replied.

★

There was a man who worked for the Post Office processing the mail that had illegible addresses.

One day, a letter came addressed in a shaky handwriting to God with no actual address. He thought he should open it to see what it was about.

The letter read:

Dear God,

I am an 80 year old widow, living on a very small pension.

Yesterday someone stole my purse. It had $100 in it, which was all the money I had until my next pension payment.

Next Sunday is Christmas, and I had invited two of my friends over for dinner. Without that money, I have nothing to buy food with, have no family to turn to, and you are my only hope. Can you please help me?

Sincerely,

Edna

The postal worker was touched. He showed the letter to the other workers. Each one dug into his or her wallet and came up with a few dollars.

By the time he made the rounds, he had collected $96, which they put into an envelope and sent to the woman. The rest of the day, all the workers felt a warm glow thinking of Edna and the dinner she would be able to share with her friends.

Christmas came and went.

A few days later, another letter came from the same old lady to God.

The workers gathered around while the letter was opened. It read:

Dear God,

How can I ever thank you enough for what you did for me?

Because of your gift of love, I was able to fix a glorious dinner for my friends.

We had a very nice day and I told my friends of your wonderful gift.

By the way, there was $4 missing.

I think it might have been those misers at the post office.

Sincerely,

Edna

FIGHTING

A small man was quietly sipping a beer in a pub when a large man approached him and hit him hard in the face. The large man said, "That's Kung Fu from China."

The little man was too stunned to speak.

Then a few minutes later while the little man was still recovering, the large man approached him again and whacked him again in the face saying, "That's Judo from Japan."

The little man was astonished. After awhile he left the bar and some time later returned. He went up to the large man who was still drinking at the bar, and gave him a whack on the face knocking him out.

The little man said to the bartender, "When he wakes up tell him, that was a shovel from Bunnings."

★

A drover from a huge cattle station in outback Australia appeared before St. Peter at the Pearly Gates.

"Have you ever done anything of particular merit?" St. Peter asked.

"Well, I can think of one thing," the drover offered. "On a trip to the backblocks of Broken Hill in New South Wales, I found a bikie gang who were threatening a young sheila. I told them to leave her alone, but they wouldn't listen. So I approached the largest and most heavily tattooed bikie and smacked him in his face, kicked his bike over, ripped out his nose ring, and threw it on the ground.

"I yelled, 'Now, back off!! Or I'll kick the shit out of the lot of ya!'"

St. Peter was impressed. "When did this happen?" "A couple of minutes ago."

★

Walking into the bar, Mike said to Charlie the bartender, "Pour me a stiff one - just had another fight with the little woman."

"Oh yeah?" said Charlie, "And how did this one end?"

"When it was over," Mike replied, "She came to me on her hands and knees."

"Really," said Charlie. "Now that's a switch! What did she say?"

She said, "Come out from under the bed, you little chicken."

FOOD

Here's the final word on nutrition and health following an exhaustive review of the research literature.

1. Japanese eat very little fat and suffer fewer heart attacks than us.

2. Mexicans eat a lot of fat and suffer fewer heart attacks than us.
3. Chinese drink very little red wine and suffer fewer heart attacks than us.
4. Italians drink excessive amounts of red wine and suffer fewer heart attacks than us.
5. Germans drink beer and eat lots of sausages and fats and suffer fewer heart attacks than us.
6. The French eat *foie-gras*, full fat cheese and drink red wine and suffer fewer heart attacks than us.

CONCLUSION: Eat and drink what you like and stop speaking English, because that's what seems to kill you.

★

After eating the main course for lunch, the children at a Catholic boarding school lined up for fruit and biscuits. In front of the large pile of apples, a nun had written a note: 'Take only ONE. God is watching.'

Behind the apples was a pile of cookies. In front of that a child had written a note: 'Take all you want. God is watching the apples.'

FOOTY

Merv has two tickets to the best seats at the MCG for the footy finals.

After he sits down, Gary comes along and asks if anyone is sitting in the seat next to him.

"No," Merv says, "that seat isn't taken."

"This is incredible!" says Gary, "who in their right mind

would have a seat like this, at the footy finals and not use it?"

Merv says, "Well, actually, the seat belongs to me. My wife was supposed to come with me, but she passed away. This is the first final we haven't been together since we got married."

"Oh... I'm sorry to hear that. That's terrible. I guess you couldn't find someone else? A friend or relative or even a neighbour to take the seat?"

Merv shakes his head. "No. They're all at the funeral."

FRENCH

Pierre, a brave French fighter pilot, takes his girlfriend, Marianne, out for a pleasant little picnic by the River Seine. It's a beautiful day and love is in the air...

Marianne leans over to Pierre and says, "Pierre, kiss me!" Pierre grabs a bottle of Merlot and splashes it on Marianne's lips.

"What are you doing, Pierre?" says the startled Marianne.

"I am Pierre, the fighter pilot! When I have red meat, I have red wine!"

She smiles and they start kissing. Things began to heat up a little and Marianne says, "Pierre, kiss me lower."

Our hero tears her blouse open, grabs a bottle of Chardonnay and pours it on her breasts.

"Pierre! What are you doing now?" asks the bewildered Marianne.

"I am Pierre, the fighter pilot! When I have white meat, I have white wine!"

She giggles and they resume their passionate interlude, and things really steam up.

Marianne leans close to his ear and whispers, "Pierre, kiss me much lower!"

Pierre rips off her underwear, grabs a bottle of Cognac and pours it in her lap. He then strikes a match and lights the Cognac.

Marianne shrieks and dives into the River Seine. Standing waist deep, Marianne throws her arms into the air and screams furiously, "Pierre what in the blazes do you think you're doing?!"

Pierre stands and says defiantly, "I am Pierre, the fighter pilot! If I go down, I go down in flames!"

★

A thief in Paris went to the Louvre Gallery. He got past security, stole several paintings, and returned safely to his van.

However, he was captured only blocks away when his van ran out of gas.

When the police inspector asked how he could mastermind such a crime and then make such an obvious error, he replied, "Inspecteur, that is the reason I stole the paintings. I had no Monet, to buy Degas, to make the Van Gogh."

The inspector replied, "Sacre bleu, 'ow did you 'ave De Gaulle to carry out the crime?"

The thief replied, "I felt I 'ad nothing Toulouse."

★

Andre from the Boules club was always boasting about knowing important people. His boules friend Guy grew sick of this. So one day, Guy said to Andre, "I don't believe you really have all these so called friends in high places." Andre was so incensed that he offered to prove these famous people were his genuine friends. He invited Guy to meet these friends, all expenses paid.

First, they visited the French president, who warmly welcomed Andre. Then they crossed the Channel and were invited to tea with the Queen of England. Guy was amazed and thought perhaps Andre wasn't a complete liar. When they were entertained by the American president, Guy was almost speechless. However, when they flew to the Vatican, Guy told Andre that this time he'd be shown up, for he knew that Andre could not know the Pope. However, Andre insisted that they go to the Pope's Sunday blessing in front of the Vatican.

He said to Guy, "Wait here and I will come out with the Pope when he blesses the crowd."

When he came out as promised, Andre thought, 'At last Guy will believe me'. He looked out in the crowd but *quelle horreur!* Guy had collapsed! Andre excused himself to the Pope and hurried down to Guy, who fortunately revived after a few moments.

"Guy was it too much for you to see that the Pope and I are such good friends?"

"Non!" said Guy. "It wasn't that. It was when the nun standing next to me, asked her friend, "Who is that bald little man next to Andre from the boules club?"

GAMBLING

One Saturday on a bad day at the race track, Colin noticed a priest stepping onto the track and blessing the forehead of one of the horses lining up for the 4th race. Amazingly that horse — who was a very long shot - won the race.

Before the next race, as the horses began lining up, Colin again saw the priest approaching a horse and blessing it on the forehead. Colin thought he couldn't do any worse than he had been all day so he put a small bet on that horse, although it was not a favourite. Sure enough it won!

When Colin saw the priest bless another horse, he rushed off to back it and was rewarded with another win. Then followed several more races before which each time the priest blessed an unpopular horse and Colin, now feeling confident, made big bets followed by wins for each long shot.

This was more exciting than any of Colin's wildest dreams and he decided to seize the moment. He withdrew all his savings from the ATM and awaited the priest's blessing.

It was clear the next race was going to be another winner because this time Colin saw the priest blessing the eyes, ears, and hooves of an old nag. So Colin placed all his money on it.

But to his dismay, he saw the old nag lurch towards the starting line and drop dead.

Colin was shocked and raced to the priest. "Father!" Colin shouted. "What's gone wrong? All day you've blessed horses who then won. But for this race, the horse you blessed has dropped dead. Because of you, I've lost all my money. I'm ruined."

The priest looked at Colin sympathetically. "My son, you must be a Protestant, because you can't tell the difference between a blessing and the Last Rites!"

GHOSTS

On a very dark night in the midst of a big storm, John Bradford, a Dublin University student, was on the side of the road hitchhiking.

The storm was so strong he could hardly see in front of him...

Suddenly, he saw a car slowly coming towards him and stop. John, desperate for shelter, jumped into the car and closed the door only to realize there was nobody behind the wheel and the engine wasn't on.

The car started moving slowly. John looked at the road ahead and saw a curve approaching. Scared, he started to pray, begging for his life. Then, just before the car hit the curve, a hand appeared out of nowhere through the window and turned the wheel. John, was paralyzed with terror, but the hand that had come through the window, had not touched or harmed him.

Shortly after John saw the lights of a pub appear down the road. Gathering strength, he jumped out of the car and ran towards the pub. Wet and out of breath, he rushed inside and started telling everybody about the horrible experience he had just had.

A silence enveloped the pub when everybody realized he was crying and... wasn't drunk.

Suddenly, the door opened, and two other people walked in from the wild, stormy night. They, like John, were also soaked and out of breath. Looking around, and seeing John Bradford sobbing at the bar, one said to the other, "Look Paddy, there's the idiot who got in the car while we were pushing it!"

GOD'S SENSE OF HUMOUR

While creating wives, God promised men that good and obedient wives would be found in all corners of the world... but He made the earth round!

★

GOLF

Bert was a keen golfer and was always the first to arrive at the course and never let illness or bad weather stop him. One day he was just about to score a birdie, when a funeral procession went past and he stopped and bent his head. Fred couldn't believe it!

"She was a good wife," explained Bert.

★

Two couples were playing golf. Ed's ball stopped right in front of a shed beside the course. His pal Mark came up with a brilliant idea to open the doors either end of the shed so that Ed could drive the ball through the shed. He took an almighty swing and the ball flew through. Unfortunately it hit his wife Amy and killed her. It was about a year before Ed began to recover from the shock.

Mark said, "Ed you've got to try to live again. Play golf with me."

Ed was very nervous but eventually gave in. However, his ball again stopped just before that shed. Bert said, "Don't worry Ed I'll open both doors."

"Don't!" screamed Ed. "That cost me a stroke last time!"

★

Tom decided to tie the knot with his long-time girlfriend Jane. One evening, after the honeymoon, he was cleaning his golf clubs in the garage. Jane was standing beside him watching. After a long silence she finally spoke, "Honey, I've been thinking, now that we're married, I think it's time you quit golfing and hanging out at the club, and drinking with your friends."

Tom looked horrified.

Jane said "Darling, what's wrong?"

Tom replied "For a minute you sounded like my ex-wife."

"Ex-wife!" Jane screamed "I didn't know you were married before!"

"I wasn't."

★

Do you know that when a woman wears a leather dress, a man's heart beats quicker, his throat gets dry, he goes weak in the knees and he begins to think irrationally.

Ever wonder why?

It's because she smells like a new golf bag.

★

Bob and Cath met at a party and Bob fell headlong in love with Cath and asked her out.

He took her to clubs, restaurants, concerts and movies and after a month he was convinced that she was the one for him.

On the anniversary of their first meeting, Bob took Cath to a beachfront restaurant. He said, "I'm very much in love with you. But there's something you must know before I ask you an important question. I must tell you that I'm obsessed with golf. I play golf, I read about golf, I watch golf on TV. I eat, sleep, and breathe golf. If that's going to be a problem for us, you'd better say so now!"

Cath looked into Bob's eyes, took a deep breath and said, "Bob I love you and I can live with that, because I love golf too. But, also I have to be totally honest with you. I'm a hooker."

Bob said, "That's probably because you're not keeping your wrists straight when you hit the ball."

★

GRANDPARENTS

"Do you believe in life after death?" the boss asks a new employee.

"I do sir," the new employee replies.

"Well, that's alright then. Because after you left early yesterday to attend your grandmother's funeral, she popped in to see you."

★

Grandma is ninety years old and still drives her own car. She writes to her granddaughter.

Dear Jeannette,

The other day I went to our local Christian book store and saw a 'Honk if you love Jesus' bumper sticker.

I was feeling particularly upbeat because I'd just been to an inspiring prayer meeting.

So, I bought the sticker and put it on my bumper.

I'm so glad I did! What an uplifting experience followed.

I had stopped at a red light at a busy intersection, lost in thought about the Lord and how good he is, and I didn't notice that the light had changed.

It's a good thing someone else loves Jesus because if he hadn't honked, I'd never have noticed.

I found that lots of people love Jesus! While I was sitting there, the man behind me started honking like crazy, and then he leaned out of his window and screamed, "For the love of God! Go! Go! Go!"

What an exuberant cheerleader he was for Jesus! Everyone started honking!

I leaned out my window and started waving and smiling at all those loving people.

I even honked my horn a few times to share in the love!

I saw one man waving in a funny way with only his middle finger stuck up in the air.

I asked your cousin Johnny who was in the back seat what that meant.

He said it was probably a good luck sign. What a lovely thought. So I leaned out the window and gave him the good luck sign right back.

Johnny burst out laughing. Even he was enjoying this religious experience!

A couple of the people were so caught up in the joy of the moment that they got out of their cars and started walking towards me.

I bet they wanted to pray or ask what church I attended, but this is when I noticed the light had changed.

So, grinning, I waved at all my brothers and sisters, and drove on through the intersection.

I noticed that I was the only car that got through the intersection before the light changed again and felt sorry that I had to leave them after all the love we had shared.

So I slowed the car down, leaned out the window and gave them all the good luck sign one last time as I drove away.

Praise the Lord for such wonderful people!

Will write again soon.

Love,

Grandma

★

I want to die asleep like my grandfather.

Not screaming in terror, like the passengers in his car.

HEALTH

Two elderly women were eating breakfast in a restaurant one morning. Ethel noticed something funny about Mabel's ear and she said, "Mabel, do you know you've got a suppository in your left ear?"

Mabel answered, "I have a suppository in my ear?" She pulled it out and stared at it. Then she said, "Ethel, I'm glad you saw this thing. Now I think I know where to find my hearing aid."

★

Many women are afraid of their first mammogram, but there's no need. By spending a few minutes doing the following exercises at home daily for a week before the exam, you'll be totally prepared.

Exercise one:
Open your refrigerator door and insert one breast in the fridge. Slam shut the door as hard as possible and lean on it. Hold that position for five seconds. Repeat again in case the first time wasn't effective enough.

Exercise two:
Go to your garage at 3 a.m. when the temperature of the cement floor is just perfect. Take off all your clothes and lie comfortably on the floor with one breast wedged under the rear tyre of the car.

Ask a friend to slowly back the car up until your breast is sufficiently flattened and chilled. Turn over and repeat with the other breast.

Exercise three:
Freeze two metal bookends overnight. Strip to the waist. Invite a stranger into the room. Ask the stranger to position the bookends on either side of one of your breasts, then to smash the bookends together as hard as she can. Repeat with the other breast. Make an appointment with the stranger to do it again next year.

★

A doctor asks a fat woman patient, "What can you fit into your busy schedule better? Exercising an hour a day or being dead 24 hours a day?"

HEARING

An elderly man called Reginald had serious hearing problems for several years. He went to a doctor who fitted him for a set of hearing aids that allowed Reginald to hear 100 percent. After a month Reginald went back to the doctor for a check and was told, "Your hearing is perfect. Your family must be really pleased that you can hear again."

Reginald replied, "Oh, I haven't told them yet. I just sit around and listen to the conversations. I've changed my will three times!"

★

Three old men are out walking. Don says, "Windy, isn't it?"

Ted replies, "No, it's Thursday!"

Pete says, "So am I. Let's get a beer."

★

Bert feared his wife Peg wasn't hearing as well as she used to and might need a hearing aid.

Not quite sure how to approach her about this, he called the family doctor to discuss the problem. The doctor told him of a simple way to check.

"Stand about 15 metres away from her, and in a normal speaking tone see if she hears you. If not, move to 10 metres, then 5 metres and so on until you get a response."

That evening, Peg was cooking dinner in the kitchen and Bert was in the study about 15 metres away. In a normal tone he asked, "Peg, what's for dinner?"

No response.

So Bert moved closer, about 10 metres from Peg and

repeated, "Peg, what's for dinner?"

Still no response.

Next, he moved into the dining room where he was about five metres from Peg and asked, "Peg, what's for dinner?" Again, he got no response.

He then walked right up behind her. "Peg, what's for dinner?"

"For goodness sake, Bert, for the FOURTH time, CHICKEN!"

★

Barry, an 85 year-old man, went to the doctor to have a check up.

Several days later, the doctor saw Barry walking down the street with a gorgeous young woman on his arm. On the following Saturday, the doctor bumped into Barry at the local footy ground and said, "You're doing great. I saw you with that gorgeous young woman."

Barry replied, "Just following your orders, Doc: 'Get a hot mamma and be cheerful.'"

"I didn't say that," replied the doctor. "I said, 'You've got a heart murmur; be careful.'"

HEAVEN AND HELL

A Catholic priest and a Pentecostal pastor arrived at the pearly gates of heaven at the same time. But instead of being warmly welcomed St Peter said, "Sorry gentlemen we're doing renovations and have temporarily run out of room."

"Help, what can we do?" asked the clerics.

"Just a moment, I have an idea," St Peter replied. He

rang the Devil in Hell and said, "Would you please do me a favour? We're doing some renovations in heaven and haven't room for the latest two residents. Could you put them up for awhile?"

"Oh alright, if you can make it worth my while," said the Devil. A price was negotiated and the two nervous men of the cloth sank down. About a week later St Peter received a call from the Devil, begging him to take the two clerics off his hands.

"Why?" asked St Peter. "Don't you have enough room?"

"Yes," said the devil, "but the priest is forgiving people and the Pentecostal pastor has raised enough money to buy air conditioning."

★

Two old mates were reflecting on life and started talking about footy. Finally they were discussing whether or not footy was played in heaven. After a while they came to an agreement. Whoever died first would come back and tell the other if they played footy in heaven.

Eventually one of the men died. About two weeks later as the other man was in bed for the night, his friend came to see him. The man asked, "Hey old mate is there footy in heaven?"

His mate answered, "I've got good news and bad news. The good news is that there is footy in heaven. The bad news is you've been selected for tomorrow's team."

HOSPITALS

Prince William visits an Edinburgh hospital. He enters a ward full of patients with no obvious sign of injury or illness and greets one.

The patient replies,

"Fair fa' your honest, sonsie face,
Great chieftain o' the pudding-race!
Aboon them a' yet tak your place,
Painch, tripe, or thairm:
Weel are ye wordy o'a grace
As lang's my airm."

The Prince is confused, so he just smiles and moves on to greet the next patient.

The patient responds,

"Some hae meat and canna eat,
And some wad eat that want it;
But we hae meat, and we can eat,
And sae let the Lord be thankit."

Even more confused, the Prince moves on to the next patient, who immediately starts to chant:

"Wee, sleekit, cowrin, tim'rous beastie,
O, what a panic's in thy breastie!
Thou need na start awa sae hasty,
Wi' bickering brattle!
I wad be laith to rin an' chase thee
Wi' murd'ring pattle!"

Now seriously troubled, the Prince turns to the accompanying doctor and asks, "Is this a psychiatric ward?"

"No," replies the doctor, "This is the serious Burns unit."

★

Hospital regulations require a wheel chair for patients being discharged. However, while working as a student nurse, I found one elderly gentleman already dressed and sitting on the bed with a suitcase at his feet, who insisted he didn't need my help to leave the hospital.

After a chat about rules being rules, he reluctantly let me wheel him to the elevator.

On the way down I asked him if his wife was meeting him.

"I don't know," he said. "She's still upstairs in the bathroom changing out of her hospital gown."

HOUSEWORK

Always keep several get well cards on the mantle-piece, so if unexpected guests arrive, they will think you've been sick and unable to clean!

★

Housework was a woman's job, but one evening, Betty arrived home from work to find the children bathed, a load of laundry in the washing machine and another in the dryer. Dinner was on the stove, and the table set.

She was astonished! It turned out that Ralph had read an article that said wives who work full-time and had to do their own housework were too tired to have sex.

The night went well and the next day, she told her office friends all about it. "We had a great dinner and Ralph even cleaned up. He helped the kids do their homework, folded all the laundry and put it away. I really enjoyed the evening."

"But what about afterwards?" asked her friends. "Oh, that

was perfect too. Ralph was too tired."

HUSBANDS & WIVES

Several men are changing in the golf club locker room. A mobile phone on a bench rings and Bob engages the hands-free speaker function and begins to talk. Everyone else in the room stops to listen.

Bob: "Hello."

Woman: "Hi darl, it's me. Are you at the club?"

Bob: "Yes."

Woman: "I'm at the shops and found this beautiful leather coat. It's only $1,000. Is it okay if I buy it?"

Bob: "Sure, go ahead if you like it that much."

Woman: "I also stopped by the Mercedes dealership and saw the latest models. There was one I really liked."

Bob: "How much?"

Woman: "$90,000."

Bob: "Okay, but for that price you'd want it with all the options."

Woman: "Great! Oh, and one more thing... I was just talking to Glenda and found out that the house I wanted last year is back on the market. They're asking $980,000 for it."

Bob: "Well, make an offer of $900,000. They'll probably take it."

Woman: "Okay. I'll see you later! I love you so much!"

Bob: "Bye!"

Bob hangs up. The other men in the locker room stare at him in astonishment, jaws dropping.

He turns and asks, "Anyone know whose phone this is?"

★

Jane stopped by unannounced at her son's house. She knocked on the door then immediately walked in. She was shocked to see her daughter-in-law, Sandra, lying on the couch, totally naked. Soft music was playing, and the aroma of perfume filled the room.

"What are you doing?" Jane asked.

"I'm waiting for Gavin to come home from work," Sandra answered.

"But you're naked!" Jane exclaimed.

"This is my love dress," Sandra explained.

"Love dress? But you're naked!"

"Gavin loves me wearing this dress," she explained. "Every time he sees me in this dress, he instantly becomes romantic and ravages me for hours."

Jane left and on her return home undressed, showered, put on her best perfume, dimmed the lights, put on a romantic CD, and lay on the couch waiting for husband Jim to arrive.

Finally, Jim came home. He walked in and saw her lying there provocatively. "What are you doing?" he asked.

"This is my love dress," she whispered, sensually.

"Needs ironing," he said. "What's for dinner?"

★

Husband, wheeling the bed with his wife in it to the kitchen says, "On your birthday, I thought you should have breakfast in bed. Can you reach the stove ok?"

★

A store that sells new husbands has opened in New York City. Among the instructions at the entrance is a description of how the store operates:

1. You may visit this store ONCE ONLY!
2. Husband Store: There are six floors and the value of the products increases as the shopper ascends the flights.

The shopper may choose any item from a particular floor, or may choose to go up to the next floor, but you cannot go back down except to exit the building!

So, a woman goes to the Husband Store to find a husband. On the first floor the sign on the door reads:

Floor 1 - These men Have Jobs.

She's intrigued, but continues to the second floor.

Floor 2 - These men Have Jobs and Love Kids.

"That's nice," she thinks, "but I want more." So she continues upward.

Floor 3 - These men Have Jobs, Love Kids, and are Extremely Good Looking.

"Wow," she thinks, but feels compelled to keep going.

Floor 4 - These men Have Jobs, Love Kids, are Drop-dead Good Looking and Help With Housework.

"Oh, mercy me!" she exclaims, "I can hardly stand it!" Still, she goes to the fifth floor.

Floor 5 - These men Have Jobs, Love Kids, are Drop-dead Gorgeous, Help with Housework, and Have a Strong Romantic Streak.

She is so tempted to stay, but she goes to the sixth floor.

Floor 6 - You are visitor 31,456,012 to this floor. There are no men on this floor. This floor exists solely as proof that women are impossible to please.

Thank you for shopping at the Husband Store.

PLEASE NOTE:

To avoid gender bias charges, the store's owner opened a New Wives store just across the street.

The first floor has wives that love sex.

The second floor has wives that love sex, have money and like beer.

The third, fourth, fifth and sixth floors have never been visited.

★

A husband and wife are shopping at their local supermarket. The husband picks up a case of beer and puts it in their cart.

"What do you think you're doing?" asks the wife. "They're on sale, only $10 for 12 cans," he replies.

"Put them back, we can't afford them," demands the wife, and so they carry on shopping.

A few aisles further along the woman picks up a $20 jar of face cream and puts it in the basket.

"What do you think you're doing?" asks the husband.

"It's my face cream. It makes me look beautiful," replies the wife.

Her husband answers, "So do 12 cans of beer and they're half the price."

★

Overworked, harassed wife sees her couch potato husband and asks him,

"What are you doing?"

"Nothing," he replies.

"But you did that yesterday."

"I haven't finished," he says.

HYGIENE

Alexei visited his 80 year old grandfather in the secluded, rural area of Tambov. After a great evening chatting, the next morning Alexei's grandfather prepared a breakfast of rye bread, sliced sausage and porridge.

However, Alexei noticed a filmy substance on his plate. He asked his grandfather,

"Are these plates clean?"

His grandfather replied, "They're as clean as cold water can get 'em. Just you go ahead and finish your meal, Alexei!"

For lunch the old man made a delicious Borsch soup and salad.

Again, Alexei was concerned about the plates, as his had tiny specks around the edge that looked like dried egg. He asked, "Are you sure these plates are clean?"

Without looking up the old man said, "I told you before, Alexei, these dishes are as clean as cold water can get them. Now don't you fret, I don't want to hear another word about it!"

Later that afternoon, Alexei was on his way to a nearby town and as he was leaving, his grandfather's dog started to growl, and wouldn't let him pass.

Alexei yelled and said, "Grandfather, your dog won't let me get to my car."

Without diverting his attention from the football game he was watching on TV, the old man shouted, "Coldwater, go lay down now, yah hear me!"

ILL HEALTH

A little old man shuffled slowly into an ice cream parlour in Naples, and pulled himself slowly, painfully, up onto a stool. After catching his breath he ordered a banana split. The waitress asked gently, "Crushed nuts?"

"No," he winced, "haemorrhoids."

★

A distraught senior citizen phoned her doctor's office.

"Is it true that the medication you prescribed has to be taken for the rest of my life?"

"Yes, I'm afraid so," the doctor replied. There was a moment of silence before the senior lady replied, "I'm wondering, then, just how serious my condition is. Because this prescription is marked 'NO REPEATS'."

INDIAN

A drunk woman, stark naked, jumped into a taxi at a Taxi Rank. The Indian driver opened his eyes wide and stared at the woman. He made no attempt to start the taxi.

"What's wrong with you Luv? Haven't you seen a naked woman before?" the woman slurred.

"I'll not be staring at you lady, I am telling you, that would not be proper, where I am coming from..."

"Well, if you're not bloody staring at me Luvie, what are you doin'?"

"Well, I am looking and looking, and I am thinking and thinking to myself, where is this lady keeping the money to be paying me with?"

★

INFIDELITY

A married man was having an affair with his secretary. One day they went to her place and made love all afternoon. Exhausted, they fell asleep and woke up at 8 pm. The man hurriedly dressed and told his lover to take his shoes outside and rub them in the grass and dirt. He put on his shoes and drove home.

"Where have you been?" his wife demanded.

"I can't lie to you," he replied. "I'm having an affair with my secretary and we had sex all afternoon."

She looked down at his shoes and said, "You liar! You've been playing golf!"

★

A mortician was working late one night. He examined the body of Mr. Blake, about to be cremated, and made a startling discovery. Blake had the largest penis he had ever seen!

"I'm sorry Mr Blake," the mortician said, "I can't let you be cremated with such an impressive penis. It must be saved for posterity."

So, he removed it, stuffed it into his briefcase, and took it home.

"I have something to show you, you won't believe," he said to his wife, opening his briefcase.

"Oh No!" his wife exclaimed, "Blake is dead!"

★

A woman was in bed with her lover when she heard her husband opening the front door.

"Hurry," she said, "stand in the corner. She rubbed baby oil all over him, then dusted him with talcum powder.

"Don't move until I tell you," she said. "Pretend you're a statue."

"What's this?" the husband inquired as he entered the room.

"Oh, it's a statue," she replied, "the Camerons bought one and I liked it so I got one for us, too."

No more was said, not even when they went to bed. Around 4 am the husband got up, went to the kitchen and returned with a sandwich and a beer.

"Here," he said to the statue, "have this. I stood like that for two days at the Cameron's and nobody offered me a damned thing."

★

For years without a break every Saturday morning Colin has got up early, quietly dressed so as not to wake his wife, picked up his golf bag and slipped quietly into the garage. This Saturday after loading his car he backed out into the torrential downpour. The gale was blowing so hard that he drove back into the garage and checked the weather on his iPhone. The forecast was the same all day. So he texted his mates and said he wouldn't be playing that day. He tiptoed back into the bedroom, undressed, and slipped back into bed. Colin nuzzled into his wife's inviting back, whispering, "The weather's dreadful."

His wife of 10 years replied, "Imagine, my idiot of a husband is playing golf in that."

INNOCENCE

Miss Finlay the 90 year old church organist was universally liked for her sweetness. One afternoon the new vicar called at her unit on his rounds. She invited him into her tiny sitting room for a cup of tea.

Looking around the room the vicar admired Miss Finlay's Allen organ. However, he was startled to see a crystal bowl filled with water sitting on top of it. Floating in the bowl was a condom!

As they shared tea and scones and the vicar became acquainted with Miss Finlay, he found it hard to stifle his curiosity. After a while pointing to the bowl he asked, "Miss Finlay, would you kindly tell me about this?"

"I'm delighted with it," she replied. "A few months ago on my daily walk through the park, I found a little package on the ground. The directions said to place it on the organ, keep it wet and it would prevent the spread of disease. Do you know I haven't been ill since."

INSULTS

Sophie's wedding day was fast approaching. Nothing could dampen her excitement -- not even her parents' nasty divorce. Her mother had found the PERFECT dress to wear and would be the best-dressed mother- of-the-bride ever!

A week later, Sophie was horrified to learn that her father's new young wife had bought the same dress! Sophie asked her to exchange it, but she refused.

"Absolutely not, I look like a million bucks in this dress,

and I'm wearing it," she replied. Sophie told her mother who graciously said, "Never mind sweetheart. I'll get another dress. After all, it's your special day." A few days later, they went shopping and did find another gorgeous dress. When they stopped for lunch, Sophie asked her mother, "Aren't you going to return the other dress? You really don't have another occasion where you could wear it."

Her mother just smiled and replied, "Of course I do, dear. I'm wearing it to the rehearsal dinner the night before the wedding."

★

- Tom asked, "What have you been doing with all the grocery money I gave you?"
  Betty replied, "Turn sideways and look in the mirror!"

- Julie asked, "How many men does it take to change a roll of toilet paper?"
  Shelly replied, "We don't know; it has never happened."

- Anna asked, "Why is it difficult to find men who are sensitive, caring and good-looking?
  Sally replied, "They already have boyfriends."

- Gigi asked, "What do you call a woman who knows where her husband is every night?"
  Greta replied, "A widow."

- Dennis asked, "Why are married women heavier than single women?"
  Nicole replied, "Single women come home, see what's in the fridge and go to bed. Married women come home, see what's in bed and go to the fridge."

IRISH

Paddy was coming through customs at the airport carrying a large bottle.

"What have you there?" said a suspicious customs officer.

"Tis Lourdes holy water. I am bringing it home with me," said Paddy.

The officer took the bottle and tried some. "Why it's Irish whiskey," he spluttered.

"Bless me," said Paddy, "another bloomin' miracle."

★

Murphy drops some buttered toast on the kitchen floor. It lands butter-side-up. He looks at this in astonishment, for he knows it's a law of nature that buttered toast always falls butter-down. He rushes to the presbytery to fetch the priest. He tells the priest that he thinks a miracle has happened at his home. He won't say what it is but wants Father Behan to see it with his own eyes. He brings Father Behan into the kitchen and asks him what he sees on the floor."

"Well," says the priest, "it's pretty obvious what we have here. Someone dropped some buttered toast, and then for some reason flipped it over so that the butter was on top."

"No, Father, I dropped it and it landed like that."

"Well," Father Behan says, "it's certainly a natural law of the universe that dropped toast never falls butter side up. But it's not for me to say it's a miracle. I'll report the matter to the Bishop, and have him send people round, to interview you, take photos, etc."

An investigation of some rigour is conducted, by priests of the archdiocese and by scientists sent from Rome. However, the final ruling is a negative. The report reads:

"It was certainly an extraordinary event that occurred in Murphy's room. Yet we have to be very cautious before ruling any happening miraculous, ruling out all possible natural explanations. In this case we have declared no miracle. For it possibly resulted from Murphy's having buttered the toast on the wrong side."

★

Calligan, a dealer from Dublin, decided to expand the line of furniture in his store, so he went to Paris to see what he could find.

After arriving in Paris, he visited some manufacturers and selected a line that he thought would sell well back home. To celebrate the new acquisition, he visited a small bistro and had a glass of wine. As he sat enjoying his wine, he noticed that the small place was quite crowded, and that the other chair at his table was the only vacant seat in the house.

Before long, a very beautiful young Parisian girl came to his table, asked him something in French (which Calligan could not understand), so he motioned to the vacant chair and invited her to sit down. He tried to speak to her in English, but she did not speak his language. After a couple of minutes of trying to communicate with her, he took a napkin and drew a picture of a wine glass and showed it to her. She nodded, so he ordered a glass of wine for her.

After sitting together for a while, he took another napkin, and drew a picture of a plate with food on it, and she nodded. They left the bistro and found a quiet cafe that featured a small group playing romantic music. They ordered dinner, after which he took another napkin and drew a picture of a couple dancing.

She nodded, and they got up to dance. They danced until the cafe closed and the band was packing up.

Back at their table, the young lady took a napkin and drew a picture of a four-poster bed.

To this day, Calligan has no idea how she figured out he was in the furniture business...

★

One Friday evening Seamus who had newly arrived in Melbourne entered Young and Jacksons pub and ordered three pints of lager. The barman lent over and said, "Mate you don't have to order several pints at once. Just order one at a time."

But Seamus explained that he'd just arrived from Dublin where he and his brothers had enjoyed a pint together each Friday for years. Now that he was in Melbourne they were continuing the practice as a way of thinking of each other. The barman thought that was fair enough and served the three pints. Seamus did this every Friday evening and he and the barman became friends.

One Friday Seamus came in and ordered only two pints. The barman was shocked but had to serve other customers before he could speak with Seamus. During a quiet spell he said "Seamus! Seamus! What's happened?"

"What do you mean?" asked Seamus.

"You've only ordered two pints what's happened to one of your brothers?"

"Oh! Nothing," Seamus laughed. "I've just given up drinking."

★

Three Irish lads were applying for the last available position on the Highway Patrol. The detective conducting the interview looked at the three of them and said, "So you all want to be policemen?"

They nodded. The detective pulled out a picture from a folder and said, "To be a detective, you have to be able to detect. You must be able to notice things such as distinguishing features and oddities like scars and so forth."

So saying, he stuck the photo in the face of the first lad and withdrew it after about two seconds. "Now," he said, "did you notice any distinguishing features about this man?"

Fergus said, "Yes, I did. He has only one eye!"

The detective shook his head and said, "Of course he has only one eye in this picture! It's a profile of his face! You're dismissed!"

Fergus hung his head and walked out of the office.

The detective then turned to Neil, stuck the photo in his face for two seconds, pulled it back, and said, "What about you? Notice anything unusual about this man?"

"Yes! He only has one ear!"

The detective put his head in his hands and exclaimed, "Didn't you hear what I just told Fergus? This is a profile of the man's face! Of course you can only see one ear! You're excused too!"

Neil shuffled off sheepishly.

The detective turned his attention to Terry and flashed the photo in his face for a couple of seconds and withdrew it, saying, "All right, did you notice anything distinguishing or unusual about this man?"

Terry said, "Sure. This man wears contact lenses." The detective frowned, took another look at the picture, and began looking at some of the papers in the folder. He looked up at

Terry with a puzzled expression and said, "You're right! His bio says he wears contacts! How in the world could you tell that by looking at his picture?"

Terry said, "Well, with only one eye and one ear, he certainly can't wear glasses."

★

ITALIAN

At lunch time two Italian secondary school students in Melbourne, Orico and Piedro, talk animatedly at a table near a female student who is reading while eating. After a few moments she loses concentration when she hears Orico saying, "Effa come first, then I come, then Ella come, then I come, then pee, then I come, then Enna then Oh come, then Arse come lasta.

The girl is shocked. She says, "I'm going to report you for your foul language and talking about your sex lives in the school canteen."

Orica says, "Hey, whate are you talking aboute? 'I'm justa helping Piedro spella Filipinos, for his geography exams."

★

An old Italian man is dying. He calls his grandson to his bedside.

"Guido, I wan' you lissina me. I wan' you to take-a my chrome plated 8 revolver so you will always remember me."

"But grandpa, I really don't like guns. How about you leave me your Rolex watch instead?"

"You lissina me, boy. Somma day you gonna be runna da business, you gonna have a beautiful wife, lotsa money, a big-a home and maybe a couple-a bambinos.

"Somma day you gonna come-a home and maybe finda you wife inna bed with anudder man.

"Whatta you gonna do then? Pointa to you Rolex and say, 'Time's up?'"

★

For two years a man was having an affair with an Italian woman. One night, she told him that she was pregnant. Not wanting to ruin his reputation or his marriage, he paid her a large sum of money to go to Italy and secretly have their child. If she stayed in Italy to raise the child, he would also provide child support until the child turned 18. She agreed, but asked how he would know when the baby was born. To keep it discreet, he told her to simply mail him a post card, and write 'Spaghetti' on the back. He would then arrange for the child support payments to begin.

One day, about eight months later, he came home to his confused wife. "Darling," she said, "you received a very strange post card today."

"Oh, just give it to me and I'll explain it later," he said. The wife obeyed and watched as her husband read the card, turned white, and fainted.

Written on the card was: *Spaghetti, Spaghetti, Spaghetti, Spaghetti, Spaghetti. Three with meatballs, two without. Send extra sauce.*

JEWISH

Several centuries ago, the Pope decreed that all the Jews had to convert to Catholicism or leave Italy. There was a huge outcry from the Jewish community, so the Pope offered a deal. He'd have a religious debate with the leader of the Jewish community. If the Jews won, they could stay in Italy. If the Pope won, they'd have to convert or leave.

The Jewish people met and picked an old and wise Rabbi to represent them in the debate. However, as the Rabbi spoke no Italian, and the Pope spoke no Yiddish, they agreed that it would be a 'silent' debate.

On the chosen day the Pope and Rabbi sat opposite each other. The Pope raised his hand and showed three fingers. The Rabbi looked back and raised one finger.

Next, the Pope waved his finger around his head. The rabbi pointed to the ground where he sat.

The Pope brought out a communion wafer and a chalice of wine. The rabbi pulled out an apple.

With that, the Pope stood up and declared himself beaten and said that the rabbi was too clever. The Jews could stay in Italy.

Later the cardinals met with the Pope and asked him what had happened.

The Pope said, "First I held up three fingers to represent the Trinity."

He responded by holding up a single finger to remind me there is still only one God common to both our beliefs.

"Then, I waved my finger around my head to show him that God was all around us.

He responded by pointing to the ground to show that God

was also right here with us.

"I pulled out the wine and water to show that God absolves us of all our sins. He pulled out an apple to remind me of the original sin. He bested me at every move and I could not continue."

Meanwhile, the Jewish community gathered to ask the Rabbi how he'd won.

"I haven't a clue," the rabbi said. "First, he told me that we had three days to get out of Italy, so I gave him the finger.

"Then he tells me that the whole country would be cleared of Jews and I told him that we were staying right here."

"And then what?" asked a woman.

"Who knows?" said the rabbi. "He took out his lunch so I took out mine."

★

A Jewish rabbi and a Catholic priest who were old friends met at the town's annual 4th of July picnic, and enjoyed their usual banter.

"This baked ham is really delicious," the priest teased the rabbi. "You really ought to try it. I know it's against your religion, but I can't understand why such a wonderful food should be forbidden! You don't know what you're missing. You just haven't lived until you've tried Mrs Miller's prized Virginia Baked Ham. Tell me, rabbi, when are you going to break down and try it?"

The rabbi looked at the priest with a big grin, and said, "At your wedding."

★

An elderly man walks into a confessional.

"I'm 90 years old and have a wonderful wife of 65 years,

eight children, 32 grandchildren, and 50 great grandchildren. Yesterday, I gave a lift to a university student. We went to a motel, where we had sex all afternoon."

Priest: "Say 10 Hail Marys and give $1,000 to the poor box."

Man: "Why?"

Priest: "For your sins."

Man: "What sins?"

Priest: "What kind of a Catholic are you?"

Man: "I'm Jewish."

Priest: "What are you doing here?"

Man: "I'm 90 years old... I'm telling everybody."

★

A man goes to see the Rabbi. "Rabbi, something terrible is happening and I have to talk to you about it."

The Rabbi asks, "What's wrong?"

The man replies, "My wife is poisoning me."

The Rabbi is very surprised and asks, "Why would she do that?"

The man then pleads, "I'm telling you, I'm certain she's poisoning me. What should I do?"

The Rabbi then offers, "Let me talk to her. I'll see what I can find out and I'll let you know."

A week later the Rabbi calls the man and says, "I spoke to your wife on the 'phone for three hours. You want my advice?"

"Yes," says the man

"Take the poison."

LEGAL FRATERNITY

A dog ran into a butcher's shop and grabbed a roast off the counter. Fortunately, the butcher recognized the dog as belonging to a neighbour of his, who happened to be a lawyer.

Incensed at the theft, the butcher called him up and said, "Hey, if your dog stole a roast from my butcher shop, would you be liable for the cost of the meat?"

The lawyer replied, "Of course, how much was the roast?"

"$7.98."

A few days later the butcher received a cheque in the mail for $7.98.

Attached to it was an invoice that read: Legal Consultation Service: $150.

★

The judge says to a double-homicide defendant, "You're charged with beating your wife to death with a hammer."

A voice at the back of the courtroom yells out, "You b.....!"

The judge says, "You're also charged with beating your mother-in-law to death with a hammer."

The voice in the back of the courtroom yells out, "You rotten b.....!"

The judge stops and says to Jack in the back of the courtroom. "Sir, I can understand your anger and frustration at these crimes, but no more outbursts from you, or I'll charge you with contempt. Is that understood?"

Jack stands up and says, "I'm sorry, Your Honour, but for fifteen years I've lived next door to that creep, and every time I asked to borrow a hammer, he said he didn't have one."

★

A lawyer is on a long flight and is bored. So he decides to have a game at the expense of the man sitting beside him.

The lawyer asks him if he would like to play a game. The man is tired and just wants to take a nap, so he politely declines, and tries to catch a few winks. The lawyer persists, and says that the game is a lot of fun.

"I ask you a question, and if you don't know the answer, you pay me only $5. You ask me one, and if I don't know the answer, I pay you $500," he says.

This catches the man's attention and to keep the lawyer quiet, he agrees to play the game. The lawyer asks the first question, "What's the distance from the Earth to the Moon?" The man doesn't say a word, reaches in his pocket, pulls out a five-dollar bill, and hands it to the lawyer.

Now, it's the man's turn. He asks the lawyer, "What goes up a hill with three legs, and comes down with four?" The lawyer uses his laptop and searches all references he can find on the Net. He sends emails to smart people he knows, but to no avail. After an hour of searching while his companion is sleeping, he gives up. He wakes up his neighbour and hands him $500. The man pockets the $500 and goes back to sleep.

The lawyer is desperate to know the answer. He wakes up the man and asks, "Well, what goes up a hill with three legs and comes down with four?"

The man reaches in his pocket, hands the lawyer $5 and goes back to sleep.

LITTLE OLD LADIES

The local doctor was making a house call to a little old lady who invited him into the sitting room and asked him to sit while she went to look for her teeth. As he waited he noticed a bowl of peanuts and helped himself to one, then another and as one does, finished the lot before he knew it. Just then the woman came back but unfortunately hadn't been able to find her teeth. The doctor was all apologies about eating all the peanuts and offered to buy her some fresh ones.

"No problems," was her mumbled, toothless reply. "At my age I only suck off the chocolate."

★

A young man shopping in a supermarket noticed a little old lady following him around. If he stopped, she stopped. And she kept staring at him. She finally overtook him at the checkout, and turned to him saying, "I hope I haven't made you feel ill at ease; it's just that you look so much like my late son."

He answered, "That's alright."

"I know it's silly, but if you'd call out 'Good bye, Mum' as I leave the store, it would make me feel so happy."

She then went through the checkout, and as she was on her way out of the store, the man called out, "Goodbye, Mum."

The little old lady waved and smiled back at him.

Pleased that he had brought a little sunshine into someone's day, the young man went to pay for his groceries.

"That comes to $121.85," said the cashier. "How come it's so much? I only bought five items."

The cashier replied, "Yeah, but your mother said you'd pay for her things, too."

LOGIC

A small boy is sent to bed by his father.

Five minutes later: "Da-ad..."

"What?"

"I'm thirsty. Can you bring a drink of water?"

"No. You had your chance. Lights out."

Five minutes later: "Da-aaaad......"

"WHAT?"

"I'm THIRSTY. Can I have a drink of water?"

"I told you NO! If you ask again, I'll have to smack you!!"

Five minutes later: "Daaaa-aaaad..."

"WHAT!"

"When you come in to smack me, can you bring a drink of water?"

★

Two young boys walked into a pharmacy one day, picked out a box of tampons and went to the checkout counter. The pharmacist asked the older boy, "Son, how old are you?"

"Eight," the boy replied.

"Do you know what these are used for?"

The boy replied, "Not exactly, but they aren't for me. They're for him. He's my brother. He's four. We saw on TV that if you use these, you would be able to swim, play tennis and ride a bike. Right now, he can't do none of those."

★

Mum was cooking pancakes for her sons, Alexander 5, and Noah 3. The boys began to argue over who would get the first pancake.

Their mother saw the opportunity for a moral lesson. "If Jesus was sitting here, He would say, 'Let my brother have the first pancake, I can wait.'"

Alexander turned to his younger brother and said, "Noah, you be Jesus!"

★

Three year old Jane was watching her mother breast-feeding her new baby brother. After a while Jane asked, "Mummy, why have you got two? Is one for hot milk and the other for cold?"

LOVE

An ad in the newspaper read: SINGLE BLACK FEMALE seeks male companionship, ethnicity unimportant. I'm a very good girl who LOVES to play. I love long walks in the woods, riding in your pickup truck, hunting, camping and fishing trips, cozy winter nights lying by the fire. Candlelight dinners will have me eating out of your hand. I'll be at the front door when you get home from work, wearing only what nature gave me. Call 03 862-0531 and ask for Daisy. I'll be waiting...

More than 10,000 men found themselves talking to the Pets Rescue Home about a six week-old black retriever cross.

★

The old man ordered one hamburger, one order of French fries and one drink. He unwrapped the plain hamburger and carefully cut it in half. He placed one half in front of his wife, then carefully counted out the French fries, dividing them into two piles and neatly placed one pile in front of his wife.

He took a sip of the drink, then his wife took a sip and then set the cup down between them. As he began to eat his few bites of hamburger, the people around them kept looking over and whispering. You could tell they were thinking, "That poor old couple – all they can afford is one meal for the two of them."

As the man began to eat his fries a young man came to the table. He politely offered to buy another meal for the old couple. The old man said they were just fine. They were used to sharing everything. The surrounding people noticed the little old lady hadn't eaten a bite. She sat there watching her husband eat and occasionally taking turns sipping the drink.

Again the young man came over and begged them to let him buy another meal for them. This time the old woman said, "No, thank you, we are used to sharing everything."

As the old man finished and was wiping his face neatly with the napkin, the young man again came over to the little old lady who had yet to eat a single bite of food and asked, "What is it you're waiting for?"

She answered, "The teeth."

MAGIC

I was walking down the road when I saw an Afghan bloke standing on a first floor balcony shaking a carpet. I shouted up to him, "What's up Mo, won't it start?"

★

A chap rubs a magic lamp and the genie offers him three wishes. He thinks for a while, then says, "I would like to be rich, I would like to be royalty, and I would like to be married to a beautiful woman."

"I wish everyone was so easy," says the genie.

Next thing he knows he's waking up in a four-poster bed with satin sheets. By him lies a gorgeous woman, her lustrous hair spread over the pillow. Suddenly she wakes, "Time to get up, Franz Ferdinand," she says, "we have to be in Sarajevo in an hour..."

★

It was entertainment night at the Senior Citizens Centre. Bernard the hypnotist explained, "I'm going to hypnotize every member of the audience."

The excitement was almost electric as Bernard withdrew a beautiful antique pocket watch from his coat.

"I want each of you to keep your eyes on this antique watch. It's a very special watch. It's been in my family for 10 generations."

He swung the watch gently back and forth while quietly chanting, "Watch the watch, watch the watch, watch the watch..."

The crowd became mesmerized as the watch swayed back and forth, light gleaming off its polished surface.

A hundred pairs of eyes followed the swaying watch until, suddenly, the chain broke; it slipped from the hypnotist's fingers and fell to the floor, breaking into a hundred pieces.

"SHIT!" said the hypnotist.

It took three days to clean up the Senior Citizens Centre.

MARRIAGE

St Peter's Catholic Church, has weekly 'Husbands' marriage seminars.

At the session last week, the priest asked Giuseppe, who said he was approaching his 50th wedding anniversary, to take a few minutes and share some insight into how he had managed to stay married to the same woman all those years.

Giuseppe replied to the assembled husbands, "Wella, I'va tried to treat her nice, spenda da money on her, but besta of all is, I tooka her to Italy for the 25th anniversary!"

The priest responded, "Giuseppe, you are an inspiration to all the husbands here! Please tell us what you are planning for your wife for your 50th anniversary?"

Giuseppe proudly replied, "I gonna go pick her upa."

★

A young couple married and went on their honeymoon. Soon after their return, the new wife Sarah rang her mother.

"Well," said her mother, "how was the honeymoon?"

"Oh Mama," Sarah replied, "it was wonderful! *So* romantic, and he's... he's..."

Suddenly she burst into tears.

"As soon as we returned, Sam started using the most horrible language. Things I'd never heard before..." sobbed Sarah.

"I mean, all these *awful* four-letter words! You've got to take me home! *Please* Mama!" Sarah wailed.

"Sarah, *Sarah!*" her mother said. "Calm down! You need to stay with your husband and work this out. Now, tell me, what could be so awful? WHAT four-letter words?"

"*Please* don't make me tell you, Mama," wept the daughter.

"I'm *so* embarrassed; they're just too awful! JUST COME GET ME... *PLEASE!*"

"Darling, baby, you must tell me what has upset you so. Tell your mother those horrible four-letter words!"

Sobbing, Sarah said, "Oh, Mama!!! He used words like: "DUST...WASH... IRON... and COOK!!!"

★

Wife: "What are you doing?"

Husband: "Nothing."

Wife: "Nothing...? You've been reading our marriage certificate for an hour."

Husband: "I was looking for the expiry date."

★

A woman's husband had been slipping in and out of a coma for several months. Yet she had stayed by his bedside every single day.

One day, when he came to, he motioned her to come nearer.

As she sat by him, he whispered, eyes full of tears, "You know what? You've been with me through all the bad times. When I was fired, you were there to support me. When my business failed, you were there. When I was shot, you were by my side. When we lost the house, you stayed right here. When my health started failing, you were still by my side...You know what May?"

"What dear?" she gently asked, smiling as her heart began to fill with warmth.

"I'm beginning to think you're bad luck..."

★

Marriage is like a deck of cards. In the beginning all you need is two hearts and a diamond. By the end, you wish you had a club and spade.

★

A man and his wife were having some problems at home and were giving each other the silent treatment. Suddenly, the man realized that the next day, he would need his wife to wake him at 5:00 am for an early morning business flight. Not wanting to be the first to break the silence (and LOSE), he wrote on a piece of paper: *Please wake me at 5:00 am.*

He left it where he knew she would find it. The next morning, the man woke up, only to discover it was 9:00 am and he had missed his flight. Furious, he was about to go and see why his wife hadn't wakened him, when he noticed a piece of paper by the bed. The paper said: *It's 5:00am. Wake up.*

MARRIED LOVE

A couple is lying in bed. The man says, "I'm going to make you the happiest woman in the world."

The woman replies, "I'll miss you."

MARRIED SEX

A wife went to see a psychiatrist and said, "I've got a big problem, doctor. Every time we're in bed and my husband climaxes, he lets out this ear splitting yell."

"My dear," the shrink said, "that's completely natural. I

don't see what the problem is."

"The problem is," she complained, "it wakes me up!"

★

A man was in a terrible accident, and his 'manhood' was mangled and torn from his body. His doctor assured him that modern medicine could give him back his manhood, but that his insurance wouldn't cover the surgery since it was considered cosmetic. The doctor said it would cost $3,500 for 'small', $6,500 for 'medium' and $14,000 for 'large'.

The man was sure he would want a medium or large, but the doctor urged him to talk it over with his wife before he made any decision. The man called his wife and explained their options. The doctor came back into the room, and found the man looking dejected.

"Well, what have you two decided?" asked the doctor.

The man answered, "She'd rather remodel the kitchen."

★

"Darling how many women have you slept with?" a woman asks her husband one day.

"Only you, darling," her husband proudly replies. "With all the others, I was awake!"

★

She was standing in the kitchen, preparing our usual soft-boiled eggs and toast for breakfast, wearing only the 'T' shirt that she normally slept in.

As I walked in, almost awake, she turned to me and said softly, "You've got to make love to me this very moment!"

My body shook and I thought, "I'm either still dreaming or

this is going to be my lucky day!"

Not wanting to lose the moment, I embraced her and then gave it my all; right there on the kitchen table.

Afterwards she said, "Thanks," and returned to the stove, her T-shirt still around her neck.

Happy, but a little puzzled, I asked, "What was all that about?"

She explained, "The egg timer's broken."

★

A married woman decided that she needed to pep up her sex life. So she arranged for the kids to stay overnight at Grandma's, she took a long scented-oil bath and then put on her best perfume. She slipped into a tight leather bodice, a black garter belt, black stockings and six-inch stilettos. She finished it off with a black mask, ready for action.

When her husband got home from work, he grabbed a beer and the remote, sat down and yelled, "Hey, Batman, what's for dinner?"

MEDICAL SPECIALISTS

Some medical friends met annually to shoot rabbits. The GP was the first to spot a rabbit. He took aim then hesitated and decided to ask for a second opinion on whether that was a rabbit or a protected species. The psychiatrist also hesitated as although he thought they were rabbits, perhaps they didn't know they were. But the surgeon didn't hesitate. He grabbed his rifle and with one shot after another killed several animals. He grabbed one to take to his friend the pathologist to confirm that it was a rabbit.

★

A gynaecologist had become fed up with malpractice insurance and was almost burned out. Hoping to try another career where skilful hands would be beneficial, he decided to become a mechanic. He signed up for evening classes at the local technical college and learned all he could.

When the time for the practical exam approached, the gynaecologist prepared carefully for weeks, and completed the exam with tremendous skill.

When the results came back, he was surprised to find that he had obtained a score of 150 percent. Fearing an error, he called the instructor, saying, "I don't want to appear ungrateful for such an outstanding result, but I was wondering if there had been an error which needed adjusting."

The instructor said, "During the exam, you took the engine apart perfectly, which was worth 50 percent of the total mark. You put the engine back together again perfectly, which is also worth 50 percent of the mark."

The instructor went on to say, "I gave you an extra 50 percent because you did all of it through the muffler."

MEDICAL

In Church the pastor asked if anyone in the congregation would like to express praise for answered prayers.

A lady stood and walked to the podium.

She said, "I have a praise. Two months ago, my husband, Don had a terrible bicycle wreck and his scrotum was completely crushed. The pain was excruciating and the doctors didn't know if they could help him."

You could hear a muffled gasp from the men in the congregation as they imagined the pain that poor Don must have experienced.

"Don was unable to hold me or the children," she went on, "and every move caused him terrible pain. We prayed as the doctors performed a delicate operation, and it turned out they were able to piece together the crushed remnants of Don's scrotum, and wrap wire around it to hold it in place."

Again, the men in the congregation were unnerved and squirmed uncomfortably as they imagined the horrible surgery performed on Don.

"Now," she announced in a quavering voice, "thank the Lord, Don is out of the hospital and the doctors say that with time, his scrotum should recover completely."

All the men sighed with relief. The pastor rose and tentatively asked if anyone else had something to say.

A man stood up and walked slowly to the podium.

He said, "I'm Don."

The entire congregation held its breath.

"I just want to tell my wife that the word is sternum."

★

Frank walked into a doctor's office and the receptionist asked him what he had.

Frank said: "Shingles."

So she wrote down his name, address, medical insurance number and told him to have a seat.

Twenty minutes later a nurse's aide came out and asked Frank what he had. Frank said, "Shingles." So she wrote down his height, weight, a complete medical history and told Frank to wait in the examining room.

A half hour later a nurse came in and asked Frank what he had. Frank said, "Shingles."

So the nurse gave Frank a blood test, a blood pressure test, an electrocardiogram, and told Frank to take off all his clothes and wait for the doctor.

An hour later the doctor came in and found Frank sitting patiently in the nude and asked Frank what he had.

Frank said, "Shingles."

The doctor asked, "Where?"

Frank said, "Outside on the truck. Where do you want me to unload 'em?"

★

A man is recovering from surgery when a nurse asks him how he's feeling. "I'm ok. But I didn't like the four-letter-word the doctor used in surgery," he answered.

"Oh dear. What did he say," asked the nurse.

"OOPS!"

★

If you have a lot of tension and a headache; follow the directions on the aspirin bottle. Take two tablets and keep away from children.

MEMORY

When I went to lunch today, I noticed an old lady sitting on a park bench sobbing her eyes out. I stopped and asked her what was wrong. She said, "I have a 22 year old husband at home. He makes love to me every morning and then gets up and makes me pancakes, sausage, fresh fruit and freshly ground coffee."

I said, "Well, then why are you crying?"

She said, "He makes me homemade soup for lunch and my favourite brownies and then makes love to me for half the afternoon."

I said, "Well, why are you crying?"

She said, "For dinner he makes me a gourmet meal with wine and my favourite dessert and then makes love to me until 2:00 a.m."

I said, "Well, why on earth are you crying?"

She said, "I can't remember where I live!"

★

Robert, 85, marries Jenny, a lovely 25 year old. Since her new husband is so old, Jenny decides that after their wedding she and Robert should have separate bedrooms, because she is concerned that her aged husband might over-exert himself if they spent the entire night together.

After the wedding festivities Jenny prepares herself for bed and the expected knock on the door.

Sure enough the knock comes, the door opens and there is Robert, her 85 year old groom, ready for action. They unite as one. All goes well, Robert takes leave of his bride, and she prepares to go to sleep.

After a few minutes, Jenny hears another knock on her bedroom door, and it's Robert, Again he is ready for more action. Somewhat surprised, Jenny consents for more coupling. When the newlyweds are done, Robert kisses his bride, bids her a fond good night and leaves.

She is set to go to sleep again, but, aha, you guessed it Robert is back again, rapping on the door and is as fresh as a 25 - year - old, ready for more 'action'. And, once more they enjoy each other.

But as Robert is about to leave again, his young bride says to him, "I'm thoroughly impressed that at your age you can perform so well and so often. I've been with guys less than a third of your age who were only good once. You are truly a great lover, Robert."

Robert, somewhat embarrassed, turns to Jenny and says, "You mean I was here already?"

★

A couple in their nineties are both having problems remembering things. During a check-up, the doctor tells them that they're physically okay, but they might want to write things down to help them remember.

Later that night, while watching TV, the old man gets up from his chair. "Want anything while I'm in the kitchen?" he asks.

"Will you get me a bowl of ice cream?"

"Sure."

"Don't you think you should write it down so you can remember it?" she asks.

"No, I can remember that."

"Well, I'd like some strawberries on top, too. Maybe you should write that down, so as not to forget it?"

He says, "I'll remember that. You want a bowl of ice cream with strawberries."

"I'd also like whipped cream. I'm certain you'll forget that, write it down?" she asks.

Irritated, he says, "I don't need to write it down, I can remember it! Ice cream with strawberries and whipped cream – for goodness sake!"

Then he toddles into the kitchen. After about 20 minutes, the old man returns from the kitchen and hands his wife a plate of bacon and eggs. She stares at the plate for a moment then asks, "Where's my toast?"

MEN

A man is driving down a road. A woman is driving from the opposite direction and as they pass each other, the woman leans out of the window and yells, "PIG!" The man immediately leans out of his window and returns the insult yelling, "SLUT!"

They each continue on their way and as the man rounds the next curve, he crashes into a huge pig in the middle of the road and dies. Thought: if only men would listen.

★

Letter to a men's helpline.

Hi Bob,

I really need your advice on a serious problem. I have suspected for some time that my wife has been cheating on me. The usual signs: if the phone rings and I answer, the caller hangs up; she goes out with the girls a lot. I try to stay awake to look out for her when she comes home but I usually fall asleep. Anyway last night about midnight I hid in the shed behind the boat. When she came home she got out of someone's car buttoning her blouse, then she took her panties out of her purse and slipped them on. It was at that moment crouched behind the boat that I noticed a hairline crack in the outboard engine mounting bracket. Is that something I can weld or do I need to replace the whole bracket?

★

Evening Classes for Men

DAY ONE

HOW TO FILL ICE CUBE TRAYS

Step by step guide with slide presentation

TOILET ROLLS: DO THEY GROW ON THE HOLDERS?

Roundtable discussion

DIFFERENCES BETWEEN LAUNDRY BASKET & FLOOR

Practicing with hamper (pictures and graphics)

DISHES: DO THEY LEVITATE/FLY TO KITCHEN SINK OR WASH BY THEMSELVES?

Debate among a panel of experts.

REMOTE CONTROL

Losing the remote control – Help line and support groups

LEARNING HOW TO FIND THINGS

Starting with looking in the right place instead of turning the house upside down while screaming – Open forum

DAY TWO

EMPTY MILK CARTONS: DO THEY BELONG IN THE FRIDGE OR THE BIN?

Group discussion and role play

HEALTH WATCH: BRINGING HER FLOWERS IS NOT HARMFUL TO YOUR HEALTH

PowerPoint presentation

REAL MEN ASK FOR DIRECTIONS WHEN LOST

Real life testimonial from the one man who did

IS IT GENETICALLY IMPOSSIBLE TO SIT QUIETLY AS SHE PARALLEL PARKS?

Driving simulation

LIVING WITH ADULTS: BASIC DIFFERENCES BETWEEN YOUR MOTHER AND YOUR PARTNER

Online class and role playing

HOW TO BE THE IDEAL SHOPPING COMPANION

Relaxation exercises, meditation and breathing techniques

REMEMBERING IMPORTANT DATES & CALLING WHEN YOU'RE GOING TO BE LATE

Bring your calendar to class

GETTING OVER IT: LEARNING HOW TO LIVE WITH BEING WRONG ALL THE TIME

Individual counsellors available

★

Why does it take one million sperm to fertilize one egg?

They don't stop to ask directions.

MEN BEWARE

A mature woman is pulled over for speeding.

Woman: "Is there a problem, officer?"

Officer: "Madam, you were speeding."

Woman: "Oh, I see."

Officer: "Can I see your licence please?"

Woman: "I'd give it to you but I don't have one."

Officer: "You don't have one?!"

Woman: "I lost it, four years ago for drunk driving."

Officer: "Can I see your vehicle registration papers please?"

Woman: "I can't do that."

Officer: "Why not?"

Woman: "I stole this car."

Officer: "Stole it?"

Woman: "Yes, and I killed and hacked up the owner."

Officer: "You what?"

Woman: "His body parts are in plastic bags in the trunk if you want to see."

The officer looks at the woman and slowly backs away to his car and calls for back up. Within minutes three police cars circle the car. A senior officer slowly approaches the car, clasping his half drawn gun.

Senior officer: "Madam, could you step out of your vehicle please!" The woman does so.

Woman: "Is there a problem sir?"

Senior officer: "One of my officers told me that you stole this car and murdered the owner."

Woman: "Murdered the owner?"

Senior officer: "Yes, could you open the trunk of your car, please?"

The woman opens the trunk, revealing nothing but an empty trunk.

Senior officer: "Is this your car, madam?"

Woman: "Yes, here are the registration papers."

The officer is stunned.

Senior officer: "My officer claims that you don't have a driving licence."

The woman digs into her handbag and pulls out a clutch purse and hands it to the officer.

The officer examines the licence and looks quite puzzled.

Senior officer: "Thank you madam, my officer told me

you didn't have a licence, that you stole this car, and that you murdered and hacked up the owner."

Woman: "Bet the liar told you I was speeding, too!"

★

A woman and a man are involved in a car accident. It's a bad one. Both of their cars are totally demolished but amazingly neither of them are hurt.

After they crawl out of their cars, the woman says, "Wow, look at our cars! There's nothing left but fortunately we're not hurt. This must be a sign from God that we should be friends and be at peace with one another."

The man replied, "I agree with you completely. This must be a sign from God!"

The woman continued, "And look, here's another miracle. My car is completely demolished but this bottle of wine didn't break. Surely God wants us to drink this wine and celebrate our good fortune."

Then she hands the bottle to the man. The man shakes his head in agreement, opens it and drinks half the bottle and then hands it back to the woman.

The woman takes the bottle, immediately puts the cap back on, and hands it back to the man.

The man asks, "Aren't you having any?"

The woman replies, "No, I think I'll just wait for the police..."

★

A married couple in their early 60s were celebrating their 40th wedding anniversary in a quiet, romantic little restaurant.

Suddenly, a tiny yet beautiful fairy appeared on their table. She said, "For being such an exemplary married couple and for being loving to each other for all this time, I will grant you each a wish."

The wife answered, "Oh, I want to travel around the world with my darling husband."

The fairy waved her magic wand and – poof – two tickets for the Queen Elizabeth II appeared in her hands.

The husband thought for a moment, "Well, this is all very romantic, but an opportunity like this will never come again. I'm sorry my love, but my wish is to have a wife 30 years younger than me."

The wife, and the fairy, were deeply disappointed, but a wish is a wish.

So the fairy waved her magic wand and – poof – the husband became 92 years old.

MEN & WOMEN

A man was sitting on the edge of the bed, observing his wife, looking at herself in the mirror.

Since her birthday was not far off he asked what she'd like to have for her birthday.

"I'd like to be twelve again," she replied, still looking in the mirror.

On the morning of her birthday, he arose early, made her a nice big bowl of Coco Pops, and then took her to Luna Park.

What a day!

He put her on every ride in the park: the Death Slide, the Corkscrew, the Wall of Fear, the Screaming Monster Roller Coaster, everything there was.

Six hours later they staggered out of the theme park. Her head was reeling and her stomach felt upside down.

He then took her to a McDonald's where he ordered her a Happy Meal with extra fries and a chocolate shake.

Then it was off to the pictures with popcorn, a huge Coca Cola, and her favourite sweets... M&M's. What a fabulous adventure!

Finally she wobbled home with her husband and collapsed into bed exhausted.

He leaned over his wife with a big smile and lovingly asked, "Well dear, what was it like being twelve again?"

Her eyes slowly opened and her expression suddenly changed. "I meant my dress size, you retard!!!"

★

Wife's Diary:

Tonight, hubby was acting strangely. We met at a restaurant for dinner. I was a bit late after shopping with friends all day, so I thought he was upset about that, but he didn't say anything about it and was very quiet.

I asked him what was wrong. He said, "Nothing." I asked him if it was my fault that he was upset. He said he wasn't upset, that it had nothing to do with me, and not to worry about it. On the way home, I told him that I loved him. He smiled slightly, and kept driving. I can't explain his behaviour I don't know why he didn't say, "I love you, too."

When we got home, I felt as if I'd lost him completely, as if he wanted nothing to do with me anymore. He just sat quietly and watched TV. He continued to seem distant and absent. Finally, with such silence I went to bed. About half an hour later, he came to bed. But he still seemed distracted and his thoughts were somewhere else. He fell asleep -- I cried. I don't know what to do. I'm almost sure that his thoughts are with someone else. My life is a disaster.

Husband's Diary:

Boat wouldn't start. Can't figure it out.

★

A couple was Christmas shopping at the mall on Christmas Eve and the mall was packed. As the wife walked through the mall she was surprised to look up and see her husband was nowhere around. She was quite upset because they had a lot to do. She called him on her mobile phone to ask where he was.

In a calm voice, he said, "Honey, you remember the jewellery store we went into about four years ago, where you fell in love with that diamond necklace that we could not afford and I told you that I would get it for you one day?"

The wife choked up and started to cry and said, "Yes, I remember that jewellery store."

He said, "Well, I'm in the bar right next to it."

★

A new sign in the Bank reads: Please note that this Bank is installing new Drive-through ATM machines enabling customers to withdraw cash without leaving their vehicles.

Customers using this new facility are requested to use the procedures outlined below when accessing their accounts.

After months of careful research, MALE & FEMALE Procedures have been developed. Please follow the Appropriate steps for your gender.'

MALE PROCEDURE:
1. Drive up to the ATM.
2. LOWER your car window.

3. Insert card into machine and enter PIN.
4. Enter amount of cash required.
5. Retrieve card, cash and receipt.
6. Raise window.
7. Drive off.

FEMALE PROCEDURE:
1. Drive up to ATM machine.
2. Reverse and back up the required amount to align car window with the machine.
3. Put hand brake on, put the window down.
4. Find handbag, remove all contents on to passenger seat to locate card.
5. Tell person on mobile 'phone you will call them back and hang up.
6. Attempt to insert card into machine.
7. Open car door to allow easier access to machine due to its excessive distance from the car.
8. Insert card.
9. Re-insert card the right way.
10. Dig through handbag to find diary with your PIN written on the inside back page.
11. Enter PIN ...
12. Press cancel and re-enter correct PIN.
13. Enter amount of cash required.
14. Check makeup in rear view mirror.
15. Retrieve cash and receipt.
16. Empty handbag again to locate purse and place cash inside.
17. Drive forward three feet.
18. Reverse back to ATM machine.
19. Retrieve card.
20. Re-empty hand bag, locate card holder, and place card into the slot provided.
21. Give dirty look to irate male driver waiting behind you.
22. Restart stalled engine and drive off.

23. Redial person on mobile 'phone.
24. Drive for three to four kilometres.
25. Release Hand Brake.

★

Jill was eating lunch at a café when Malcolm, a tall, exceptionally handsome, extremely sexy, middle-aged man entered. He was so striking that she couldn't take her eyes off him.

This seasoned yet playful heartthrob noticed her overly attentive stare and walked directly toward her. Before she could apologise for staring so rudely, he leaned over and whispered to her, "I'll do anything, absolutely anything, that you want me to do, no matter how kinky, for $20.00... on one condition..."

Flabbergasted but intrigued, Jill asked what the condition was. Malcolm replied, "You have to tell me what you want me to do in just three words."

Jill considered his proposition for a moment, and then slowly removed a $20 bill from her purse, which she pressed into Malcolm's hand along with her address.

She looked deeply and passionately into his eyes, barely concealing her anticipation and excitement, and slowly and meaningfully said... "Clean My House!"

MEN & SEX

"I'm a very naughty girl," she murmured with heaving breasts, whip and biting her lip. "I need to be punished."

So he invited his mother to stay for the weekend.

★

MEXICAN

President Gomez of Mexico has announced that Mexico will not participate in the next Summer Olympics.

He said, "Anyone who can run, jump, or swim has already left the country."

MODERN LIFE

My thanks to all those dear friends and family who have sent us emails this past year.

We must thank whoever sent us the one about cockroach eggs in the glue on envelopes because we now have to use a wet towel with every envelope that needs sealing.

I no longer open a bathroom door without using a paper towel, or have the waitress put lemon slices in my ice water without worrying about the bacteria on the lemon peel.

Also, we now have to scrub the top of every can we open for the same reason.

I can't sit down on the hotel bedspread because I can only imagine what has happened on it since it was last washed.

I have trouble shaking hands with someone who has been driving because the number one pastime while driving alone is picking one's nose.

Eating a little snack sends me on a guilt trip because I can only imagine how many gallons of trans fats I have consumed over the years.

I can't touch any woman's purse for fear she has placed it on the floor of a public toilet.

I no longer worry about my soul because I have 534,201

angels looking out for me.

We no longer have any savings because we gave them to a sick girl (Debbie Marshall, who is about to die in hospital for the 1,203,562nd time).

We no longer have any money at all, but that will change according to the senior bank clerk in Kenya who wants to split $5 million with us for pretending to be a long lost relative of a customer who died intestate.

We no longer use cancer-causing deodorants even though we smell like orangutans on a hot day.

Thanks to you, we have learned that our prayers are only answered if we forward emails to nine of our friends and make a wish within two minutes.

I can't have a drink in a bar because I'll wake up in a bathtub full of ice with my kidneys gone.

We no longer can buy petrol without taking a man along to watch the car so a serial killer won't crawl in our back seat while we're filling up.

I no longer buy cookies from the supermarket since I now have their recipe.

We no longer go to shopping malls because someone will drug us with a perfume sample and rob us.

We no longer answer the 'phone because someone will ask us to dial a number for which we will get a 'phone bill with calls to Argentina, Rwanda and Uzbekistan.

Thanks to you, we can't use anyone's toilet but ours because a big, brown, African spider is lurking under the seat to cause us instant death when it bites our rear end.

I no longer use Cling Wrap in the microwave because it causes seven different types of cancer.

And thanks for letting me know I can't boil a cup of water

in the microwave anymore because it will blow up in my face – disfiguring me for life.

I no longer go to the pictures because I could be pricked with a needle infected with AIDS when I sit down.

I can't do any gardening because I'm afraid I'll get bitten by the Violin Spider and my hand will fall off.

And thanks to your great advice, we can't pick up the $5.00 we found dropped in the car park because it was probably placed there by a sex molester waiting under our car to grab our leg.

If you don't send this email to at least 861 people in the next 55 minutes, a large dove with diarrhoea will land on your head at 4pm this afternoon and the fleas from 8 camels will infest your back, causing you to grow a hairy hump.

We know this will occur because it actually happened to a friend of ours' next door neighbour's ex-mother-in-law's second husband's cousin's shopkeeper.

Oh, by the way... a scientist after a lengthy study has discovered that people with low IQ who don't have enough sex, always read their emails while holding the mouse. Don't bother taking it off now, it's too late.

★

As a woman passed her daughter's closed bedroom door, she heard a strange buzzing noise coming from within. Opening the door, she observed her daughter with a vibrator.

Shocked, she asked, "What in the world are you doing?"

The daughter replied, "Mum, I'm 35 years old, unmarried, and this thing is about as close as I'll ever get to a husband. Please, go away and leave me alone."

The next day, the girl's father heard the same buzz coming from the other side of the closed bedroom door. Upon entering the room, he observed his daughter making passionate love to her vibrator.

To his query as to what she was doing, the daughter said, "Dad I'm 35, unmarried, and this thing is about as close as I'll ever get to a husband. Please, go away and leave me alone."

A couple of days later, the wife came home from shopping, placed the groceries on the kitchen bench, and heard that buzzing noise coming from, of all places, the lounge room. She went there and saw her husband sitting on the couch, downing a cold beer, and staring at the TV.

The vibrator was next to him on the couch, buzzing like crazy. The wife asked, "What on earth are you doing?"

The husband replied, "I'm watching football with my son-in-law."

MONEY

Dan was a single guy living at home with his father and working in the family business.

When he found out he was going to inherit a fortune when his elderly father died, he decided he needed to find a wife with whom to share his fortune.

One evening, at an investment meeting, he spotted the most beautiful woman he'd ever seen. She took his breath away.

"I may look like an ordinary guy," he said to her. "But in a few years my father will die and I will inherit $200 million."

Impressed, the woman asked for his business card and one week later, she became his stepmother.

★

During the Global Financial Crisis it was important to know the difference between a seagull and a stockbroker. A seagull could still make a deposit on a Mercedes...

★

A father walks into a restaurant with his young son. He gives the boy three coins to play with to keep him occupied.

Suddenly, the boy starts choking and going blue in the face. The father realises the boy has swallowed the coins and starts slapping him on the back.

The boy coughs up two of the coins, but keeps choking. The father panics and shouts for help.

An attractive, serious looking woman, in a blue business suit is sitting at a coffee bar reading a newspaper and sipping a cup of coffee. At the sound of the commotion, she looks up, puts her coffee cup down, neatly folds the newspaper and places it on the counter, gets up from her seat and makes her way, unhurriedly, across the restaurant.

Reaching the boy, the woman carefully drops his pants; takes hold of the boy's testicles and starts to squeeze and twist, gently at first and then ever so firmly. After a few seconds the boy convulses violently and coughs up the last coin, which the woman deftly catches in her free hand.

Releasing the boy's testicles, the woman hands the coin to the father and walks back to her seat at the coffee bar without saying a word.

As soon as he is sure that his son has suffered no ill effects, the father rushes over to the woman and thanks her saying, "I've never seen anybody do anything like that before, it was fantastic. Are you a doctor?"

"No," the woman replied: "I'm with the Tax Department."

★

The parish priest was preoccupied with how he was going to ask the congregation to come up with more money than they were expecting, for repairs to the church building. Therefore, he was annoyed to find that the regular organist was sick and a substitute had been brought in at the last minute. The substitute wanted to know what to play.

"Here's a copy of the service," he said impatiently. "But, you'll have to think of something to play after I make the announcement about the finances."

During the service, the parish priest paused and said, "Brothers and sisters, we are in great difficulty; the roof repairs cost twice as much as we expected and we need $6,000 more. Any of you who can pledge $200 or more, please stand up!"

At that moment, the substitute organist played the National Anthem... And that is how the substitute became the regular organist!

MONKS

A man is driving down the road and his car breaks down near a monastery. He goes to the monastery, knocks on the door, and says, "My car broke down. Do you think I could stay the night?"

The monks graciously accept him, feed him dinner, even fix his car. As the man tries to fall asleep, he hears a strange beautiful sound. A sound like nothing he's heard before. The Sirens that nearly seduced Odysseus into crashing his ship come to his mind. He doesn't sleep that night. He tosses and turns trying to work out what could possibly be making such a seductive sound.

The next morning, he asks the monks what the sound was, but they say, "We can't tell you. You're not a monk."

Disappointed, the man leaves.

Years pass and the man is still haunted by that sound so he returns to the monastery and pleads for the answer again.

The monks reply, "We can't tell you. You're not a monk."

The man says, "If the only way I can find out what is making that beautiful sound is to become a monk, then please, make me a monk."

The monks reply, "You must travel the earth and tell us how many blades of grass there are and the exact number of grains of sand. When you find these answers, you will have become a monk."

The man sets about his task.

After years of searching he returns as a grey-haired old man and knocks on the door of the monastery. A monk answers. He is taken to a gathering of all the monks.

"In my quest to find what makes that beautiful sound, I travelled the earth and have found what you asked for; by design, the world is in a state of perpetual change. Only God knows what you ask. All a man can know is himself, and only then if he is honest and reflective and willing to strip away self-deception."

The monks reply, "Congratulations. You have become a monk. We shall now show you the way to the mystery of the sacred sound."

The monks lead the man to a wooden door, where the head monk says, "The sound is beyond that door."

The monks give him the key, and he opens the door. Behind the wooden door is another door made of stone. The man is given the key to the stone door and he opens it, only to find a door made of ruby. And so it goes as he passes through doors of emerald, pearl and diamond.

Finally, they come to a door made of solid gold. The sound has become very clear and definite. The monks say, "This is the last key to the last door."

The man can hardly breathe with excitement. His life's wish is behind that door! With trembling hands, he unlocks the door, turns the knob, and slowly pushes the door open. Falling to his knees, he is utterly amazed to discover the source of that haunting and seductive sound...

But, of course, I can't tell you what it is because you're not a monk.

MORALITY TALE

For homework a teacher told her class of 12 year olds to ask their parents to tell them a story with a moral at the end.

The next day the kids came back and one by one began to tell their stories.

Karl said, "My father's a farmer and we have a lot of egg-laying chooks. One time we were taking our eggs to market in a basket on the front seat of the car when we hit a big bump in the road and all the eggs went flying and broke and made a mess."

"What's the moral of the story?" asked the teacher.

"Don't put all your eggs in one basket!" "Very good," said the teacher.

Next little Emily raised her hand and said, "Our family are farmers too. But we raise chooks for the meat market. One day we had a dozen eggs, but when they hatched we only got ten live chicks and the moral of this story is, 'Don't count your chickens before they're hatched.'"

"That was a fine story Emily. Mick, do you have a story to share?"

"Yes. My dad told me this story about my Aunty Cheryl. Aunty Cheryl was a flight engineer on a plane in the Gulf War and her plane got hit. She had to bail out over enemy territory and all she had was three bottles of rum, a machine gun and a machete.

"She drank all the rum on the way down so it wouldn't break and then she landed right in the middle of 100 enemy troops. She killed seventy of them with the machine gun until she ran out of bullets. Then she killed twenty more with the machete until the blade broke. And then she killed the last ten with her bare hands."

"Good heavens," said the horrified teacher, "what kind of moral did your father tell you from that horrible story?"

"Stay right away from Aunty Cheryl when she's been on the grog!"

MOTHERS

Our mother taught us RELIGION: "You'd better pray that comes out of the carpet."

Our mother taught us LOGIC: "If you fall out of that swing and break your neck, you're not going to the shops with me."

Our mother taught us FORESIGHT: "Make sure you wear clean underwear in case you're hit by a bus."

Our mother taught us IRONY: "Keep crying and I'll give you something to cry about."

Our mother taught us about STAMINA: "You'll sit there

until all that spinach is finished."

Our mother taught us about WEATHER: "It looks like a tornado has been through your room."

Our mother taught us about JUSTICE: "One day you'll have kids and I hope they turn out just like you!"

Our mother taught us about ANTICIPATION: "Just wait until your father gets home."

★

Mrs Ravioli visits her son Tony for dinner. He lives with a female flatmate, Maria.

During the course of the meal, Mrs Ravioli notices how pretty Maria is.

As the evening goes on she watches Tony and Maria interact and starts to wonder if there is more between Tony and his flatmate than meets the eye.

Reading his mother's thoughts, Tony volunteers, "I know what you must be thinking, but I assure you, Maria and I are just flatmates."

About a week later, Maria came to Tony saying, "Ever since your mother came to dinner, I've been unable to find the silver sugar bowl. You don't suppose she took it, do you?"

"Well, I doubt it, but I'll email her, just to be sure."

He wrote:

Dear Mama,

I'm not saying that you 'took' the sugar bowl from my house. I'm not saying that you 'didn't take' it. But it's been missing ever since you were here for dinner.

Your Loving Son

Tony

Several days later, Tony received a response email from his

mother which read:

Dear son,

I'm not saying that you 'do' sleep with Maria, and I'm not saying that you 'do not' sleep with her.

But the fact remains that if she was sleeping in her OWN bed, she would have found the sugar bowl by now.

Your Loving

Mama

MOTHERS-IN-LAW

One year, a husband decided to buy his mother-in-law a cemetery plot as a Christmas gift.

The next year, he didn't buy her a gift. When she asked him why, he replied, "Well, you still haven't used the gift I bought you last year!"

★

I bought my mother-in-law a chair, but she won't plug it in.

★

My mother-in-law is visiting for a week. I had to clear out half my cupboard so she could have a place to hang upside down and sleep.

MULTINATIONAL

In heaven the cooks are Italian, the engineers are German, the comedians are English, the novelists are Russians and the Swedes are in charge.

In hell, the comedians are German, the cooks are English, the mechanics are Russian, the novelists are Swedes and the Italians are in charge.

★

A world-wide survey conducted by the UN consisted of only one question: "Would you please give your Honest Opinion about solutions to the food shortage in the rest of the world?"

The survey was a huge failure. In Africa they didn't know what 'food' meant. In India they didn't know what 'honest' meant. In Europe they didn't know what 'shortage' meant. In China they didn't know what 'opinion' meant. In the Middle East they didn't know what 'solution' meant. In South America they didn't know what 'please' meant, and in the USA they didn't know what 'the rest of the world' meant!

★

A big earthquake with the strength of 8.1 on the Richter scale has hit Pakistan. Two million Pakistanis have died and over a million are injured. The country is totally ruined and the government doesn't know where to start to rebuild. The rest of the world is in shock.

The USA is sending troops to help.

Saudi Arabia is sending oil.

Latin American countries are sending supplies.

New Zealand is sending sheep, cattle and food crops.

Asian countries are sending labour to assist in rebuilding infrastructure.

Australia is sending medical teams and supplies.

Britain, not to be outdone, is sending two million

replacement Pakistanis.

NEW ZEALANDERS

Two New Zealanders holidaying in Melbourne see a sign in a shop that suits are $5 each, shirts $2 and trousers $2.50 per pair.

One says to the other, "Hey we could buy some and make a fortune. Let's go in but you be quiet. I'll do the talking because if they know we come from New Zealand, they mightn't be nice to us so I'll speak in my best Aussie accent."

They enter and the first man says, "Hi mate, I want to buy 50 suits, 100 shirts and 50 trousers. I'll back up me ute and..."

The owner interrupts, "You're from New Zealand aren't you?"

"Yes. How did you know?"

"Because this isn't a menswear shop. It's a drycleaners."

NUNS

Mother Superior called a special meeting of all the convent nuns. "Sisters," she said, "we have a case of gonorrhea in the convent."

"That's great," said an 80 year old nun. "I'm tired of sauvignon blanc."

★

The 90 year old Mother Superior lay dying. The nuns stood by her bed making her comfortable and praying. They offered her milk to drink but the Mother refused it.

One of the nuns had an idea that might help. She went to the kitchen and added whisky, which was kept for special occasions, to the milk.

She returned and supported the weak Mother while holding the glass to her lips. The Mother took a tiny sip, then rallied enough to drink more. With each drink, she seemed to regain strength and finally polished off every drop.

Heartened by the Mother's improvement the nuns gathered closer and asked if she had one more message for them before she went to her heavenly home.

She looked at them with brightened eyes and said, "Don't sell that cow!"

OBEDIENCE

Five year old Ted stuck his head in the back door from the garden and screamed, "Mum! Mum!"

Mother reading in the lounge room at the other side of the house called back. "Ted don't shout across the house. Walk to the lounge room where I am and speak to me."

Ted did as he was told and walked through the lounge room. "Mum I stepped in dog poo, where's the hose?"

OLD AGE

I recently went to the new GP for a general check-up. He said I was doing 'fairly well' for my age. Hmmmm - I'm 61.

A little concerned about that comment, I asked, "Do you think I'll live to be 85?"

He asked, "Do you smoke tobacco, or drink beer, wine or hard liquor?"

"I hardly drink grog these days and don't smoke," I replied. "I'm not doing drugs, either!"

Then he asked, "Do you eat rib-eye steaks, fatty roasts and barbecued ribs?"

"I said, "Not much... my former doctor said that fatty meats are unhealthy!"

"Do you spend much time in the sun, or like playing golf, boating, surfing, hiking, or cycling?"

"No, I don't," I said.

He asked, "Do you gamble, drive fast cars, or have lots of sex?"

"No."

The doctor looked at me and said, "Then, why exactly do you want to live to 85?"

★

Arthur is 85 years old. He's played golf every day since he retired 20 years ago. One day he arrives home looking downcast.

"That's it," he tells his wife. "I'm giving up golf. My eyesight is so bad. Once I've hit the ball, I can't see where it goes."

His wife sympathises. Then she suggests: "Why don't you take my brother with you, and give it one more try."

"That's no good," sighs Arthur. "Your brother is 92. He can't help."

"He may be 92" says the wife, "but his eyesight is perfect."

So the next day, Arthur heads off to the golf course with his brother-in-law.

He tees up, takes an almighty swing, and squints down the fairway.

He turns to the brother-in-law. "Did you see the ball?"

"Of course I did!", says the brother-in-law. "I have perfect eyesight."

"Where did it go?" asks Arthur.

"Can't remember."

★

PERKS OF BEING OVER 75
1. Kidnappers are not very interested in you.
2. In a hostage situation you're likely to be released first.
3. No one expects you to run - anywhere.
4. People call at 9 pm and ask, "Did I wake you?"
5. People no longer view you as a hypochondriac.
6. There's nothing left to learn the hard way.
7. Things you buy now won't wear out.
8. You can eat dinner at 4 pm.
9. You can live without sex but not your glasses.
10. You get into heated arguments about pension plans.
11. You no longer think of speed limits as a challenge.
12. You quit trying to hold your stomach in no matter who walks into the room.
13. You sing along with elevator music.
14. Your eyes won't get much worse.
15. Your investment in health insurance is finally beginning to pay off.
16. Your joints are more accurate meteorologists than the national weather service.
17. Your secrets are safe with your friends because they can't remember them either.
18. Your supply of brain cells is finally down to manageable size.

★

OOPS

A pirate walked into a bar, and the bartender said, "Hey, I haven't seen you in a while. What happened? You look terrible."

"What do you mean?" said the pirate, "I feel fine."

"What about the wooden leg? You didn't have that before."

"Well," said the pirate, "We were in a battle, and I got hit with a cannon ball, but I'm fine now."

The bartender replied, "Well, OK, but what about that hook? What happened to your hand?"

The pirate explained, "We were in another battle. I boarded a ship and got into a sword fight. My hand was cut off. I got fitted with a hook but I'm fine, really."

"What about that eye patch?"

"Oh," said the pirate, "One day we were at sea, and a flock of birds flew over. I looked up, and one of them pooped into my eye."

"You're kidding," said the bartender. "You couldn't lose an eye just from bird poop."

"It was my first day with the hook."

OUT OF THE MOUTH OF BABES

The preacher's six year-old daughter noticed that her father always paused and bowed his head for a moment before starting his sermon. One day, she asked him why.

"Well sweetie," he began, proud that his daughter was so observant of his messages. "I'm asking the Lord to help me preach a good sermon."

"How come He doesn't answer?" she asked.

★

The young couple invited their elderly pastor for Sunday dinner. While they were in the kitchen preparing the meal, the minister asked their five year old son what they were having.

"Goat," the little boy replied.

"Goat?" replied the startled man of the cloth, "Are you sure about that?"

"Yes," said the youngster. "I heard Daddy say to Mummy, 'Today is just as good as any to have the old goat for dinner.'"

★

Four year old Jeannette asked her mother if she could play outside with the boys next door.

Mum said, "No you can't play with the boys. They're too rough."

Jeanette thought about this for a while then asked, "If I can find a smooth one, can I play with him?"

PARENTHOOD

A single mother fills in a child support document at Centrelink and says she has 12 children. She notes their names: the oldest is Peter, next is Peter, next is a girl called Peta, and the next two are called Peta, then the next is a boy called Peter and so on.

The clerk notes this and says, "Ah I see a pattern here. Do you have any children who are not called Peter or Peta?"

"No," says the woman all the boys are called Peter and all the girls, Peta."

"Why have you done this?" asks the clerk.

"It's very handy," says the mother. "When I want them to get up I just call out one name or if I want them to come to dinner or to go and catch the bus to school and so on."

"But what if you just wanted to speak to one child?" asked the clerk.

"Oh then I call them by their surname," said the mother.

★

You spend the first two years of their life teaching them to walk and talk. Then you spend the next sixteen telling them to sit down and shut up

★

The main purpose of holding children's parties is to remind yourself that there are children more awful than your own.

★

Be nice to your kids. They will choose your nursing home one day.

PARENTHOOD JOYS

The boss of a new employee needs to call him at home about an urgent problem with one of the main computers. After dialing he's greeted by a child's whisper, "Hello."

"Is your daddy home?" he asked.

"Yes," whispered the small voice.

"May I talk with him?"

"No," whispers the child.

Surprised, the boss asked, "Is your mummy there?"

"Yes."

"May I talk with her?"

Again the small voice whispered, "No."

Hoping there was somebody with whom he could leave a message, the boss asked, "Is anyone else there?"

"Yes," whispered the child, "a policeman."

Wondering what was going on the boss asked, "May I speak with the policeman?"

"No, he's busy," whispered the child.

"Busy doing what?"

"Talking to Mummy and Daddy and the Fireman," came the whispered answer.

Growing worried as he heard what sounded like a helicopter the boss asked, "What's that noise?"

"A hello-copper," answered the whispering voice.

"What's going on?" the boss asked alarmed.

In an awed whisper the child answered, "The search team just landed the hello-copper."

"Really worried now, the boss asked, "What are they searching for?"

"Me!"

PARROTS

A woman went to a pet shop and spotted a large, beautiful parrot. A sign on the cage said $10.

"Why so cheap?" she asked the pet store owner. The owner

said, "Well, I should tell you that this bird used to live in a brothel and sometimes says some pretty vulgar stuff."

The woman thought about this, but decided she wanted the bird anyway.

She took it home and hung the bird's cage up in her living room and waited for it to say something. The bird looked around the room, then at her, and said,

"New house, new madam."

The woman was a bit shocked at the implication, but then thought, 'that's really not so bad.' When her two teenage daughters returned from school, the bird looked at them and said, "New house, new madam, new girls."

The girls and the woman were a bit offended but then began to laugh about the situation considering how and where the parrot had been raised.

Soon after, the woman's husband Keith came home from work.

The bird looked at him and said, "Hi Keith!"

★

John received a parrot as a gift. The parrot had a bad attitude and an even worse vocabulary. Every word out of the bird's mouth was rude and obnoxious. John tried and tried to change the bird's attitude by consistently saying only polite words, playing soft music and anything else he could think of to 'clean up' the bird's vocabulary.

Finally, John was fed up and yelled at the parrot. The parrot yelled back. John shook the parrot and the parrot got angrier and even ruder. In desperation, John grabbed the bird and put him in the freezer. The parrot squawked and kicked and screamed.

Then suddenly, there was total quiet. Not a peep for more than a minute.

Fearing that he'd hurt the parrot, John opened the freezer door. The parrot calmly stepped out and said, "I believe I may have offended you with my rude language and actions. I'm sincerely remorseful for my inappropriate transgressions and I fully intend to do everything I can to correct my rude and unforgivable behaviour."

John was stunned at the change in the bird's attitude.

As he was about to ask the parrot what had made such a dramatic change in his behaviour, the bird spoke, very softly.

"May I ask, what did the turkey do?"

★

Barbara's dishwasher broke down so she called in a repairman. As she had to go to work the next day, she told the repairman, "I'll leave the key under the mat. Fix the dishwasher, leave the bill on the counter, and I'll mail you a cheque. Oh, by the way don't worry about my dog Spike. He won't bother you. But, whatever you do, do NOT, under ANY circumstances, talk to my parrot! I must stress – do not talk to my parrot!"

When the repairman arrived at Barbara's apartment the following day, he discovered the biggest, meanest looking dog he had ever seen. But, just as she had said, the dog lay there on the carpet watching the repairman go about his work.

The parrot, however, drove him nuts with his incessant yelling, cursing and name calling. Finally the repairman couldn't stand it any longer and yelled, "Shut up, you stupid, ugly bird!"

To which the parrot replied, "Get him Spike!"

PARTIES

A little boy was watching his parents dress for a party. When he saw his dad donning his dinner jacket, he warned, "Daddy, you shouldn't wear that suit."

"Why not Tim?"

"It always gives you a headache the next morning."

PETS

A lonely guy decides to buy a pet to bring more fun to his life. So he goes to the pet shop and asks the owner for an unusual pet. After some discussion he buys a centipede, which comes in a little white box to use for his house.

He takes the box home and decides he will start by taking his new pet to the bar for a drink. So he asks the centipede in the box, "Would you like to go to the local pub with me and have a beer?" But there is no answer from his new pet. This bothers him a bit, so he waits a few minutes and then asks again, "How about going to the bar and having a drink with me?"

Again there is no answer from his new friend and pet. He decides to ask him one more time. This time putting his face up against the centipede's house and shouting, "Hey, in there! Would you like to go to the local pub and have a drink with me?"

Then he hears a little voice from the box, "I heard you the first time! I'm just putting my shoes on!"

★

Rules for the cat.

The cat is not allowed on the furniture. Alright the cat can go on the furniture, but NOT on the kitchen counter.

OK the cat can go on the kitchen counter too, just not when I'm preparing food. Deal?

Fine…The cat can go wherever it wants, whenever it wants, as long as it doesn't swat me in the face at 5.30 in the morning demanding to be fed...

The cat will be fed at 5.30 in the morning.

PHONE CALLS

Larry, an American, decided to write a book about famous churches around the world. He started in New York and at the cathedral he noticed a golden telephone mounted on the wall with a sign that read: $10,000 per call. Intrigued, Larry asked a priest what the telephone was used for.

The priest replied that it was a direct line to heaven and that for $10,000 you could talk to God.

Larry thanked the priest and next visited the Columbian capital Bogota where at a famous cathedral, he saw the same golden telephone with the same sign under it. He wondered if it was used for the same purpose as he'd seen in New York. So he asked a nun. She said that it was a direct line to heaven and that for 10,000 pesos he could talk to God.

"Thank you," said Larry. He then travelled to capital cities of other countries in South America, Europe, Africa and Asia. In every famous church he saw the same golden telephone with the same '10,000 per call' in the local currency. Finally, he went to Canberra, Australia. Sure enough in the first church he entered, there was the same golden telephone, but this time the sign under it read: '25 cents per call'.

Larry was surprised so he asked the priest about the sign. "Father, I've travelled all over the world and I've seen this same golden telephone in many churches. I'm told that it's a direct line to Heaven, but in every country the price is $10,000 or equivalent per call. Why is it so cheap here?"

The priest smiled and answered, "You're in Australia now, son – it's a local call."

★

"Hello?"

"Hi Sweetie, this is Daddy. Is Mummy near the phone?"

"No Daddy, she's upstairs in the bedroom with Uncle Paul."

After a brief pause, Daddy says, "But Sweetie, you haven't got an Uncle Paul."

"Oh yes I have, and he's upstairs in the bedroom with Mummy, right now."

Brief pause. "Uh, okay then, this is what I want you to do. Put the 'phone down on the table, run upstairs, go to the bedroom and shout to Mummy that Daddy's car just pulled into the driveway. Then come back to the 'phone."

"Okay Daddy, just a minute."

A few minutes later the little girl comes back to the phone. "I did it Daddy."

"And what happened Sweetie?"

"Well, Mummy jumped out of bed with no clothes on and ran around screaming. Then she tripped on the rug, hit her head on the dressing table and now she isn't moving at all!"

"Oh NO! What about Uncle Paul?"

"He jumped out of bed with no clothes on, too. He jumped

out of the window and into the swimming pool. But I guess he didn't know that you took out the water last week to clean it. He hit the bottom of the pool and I think he's dead."

Long pause.

Longer pause.

Even longer pause

Then Daddy says, "Swimming pool? Is this 9228 5731...?"

POLISH

Zigmunt Adamski a Pole, moved to Australia and about a year later married a local girl. After a few months he visited a solicitor Edward Blamey, and said he wanted a divorce – fast.

Blamey said, "You'll have to answer some questions first. What are your grounds?"

Adamski: "A quarter acre block, close to station."

Blamey: "No, I mean what is the foundation of this case?"

Adamski: "Timber piles."

Blamey: "That's not what I'm asking. What is your grudge?"

Adamski: "We haf carport."

Blamey: "I mean, what are your relations like?"

Adamski: "My relations all dead."

Blamey: "Is there any infidelity in your marriage?"

Adamski: "We have hi-fidelity stereo and goot DVD player."

Inwardly groaning, Blamey thought, this is going to be a long session.

"Look, does your wife beat you up?"

Adamski : "No, I always up before her."

Blamey: "Is your wife a nagger?"

Adamski: "No, she white."

Blamey was mystified: "Why do you want this divorce?"

Adamski: "She going to kill me."

"Why do you think that?"

Adamski: "I got proof."

"What proof?"

Adamski: "She going to poison me. She buy bottle at pharmacy and put it on bathroom shelf. I read it and it say: *Polish Remover*."

POLITICS

Tony Abbott is visiting the UK and is impressed by the charisma of the royal family so he asks the Queen for the secret.

She replies that she keeps them on their toes by asking challenging questions.

The Duke of Edinburgh passes by and the Queen asks, "Phillip if your mother had a child but it isn't your brother or your sister, who is it ?'

Phillip says, "That's easy. It's **me**."

"Correct," says the Queen. Tony is impressed.

Back in Australia, Tony tries this with the treasurer Joe Hockey.

"Joe, if your mother has a child but it is not your brother or your sister, who is it?"

Joe is puzzled, so says he will ask the smartest parliamentarian, Clive Palmer.

"Clive, your mother has a child but it is not your brother or your sister, who is it?" Clive replies, "I'm glad you've asked me for guidance Joe, of course the answer is **me**."

Joe scuttles back to Tony. "Tony, I have the answer to that

brother and sister poser, the answer is Clive Palmer!"

Tony sarcastically replies, "We mustn't let the electorate know Joe, but you're a moron. It's obvious that the answer is the Duke of Edinburgh."

★

While crossing the road, a well-known politician is hit by a dunny truck and dies. His soul arrives in heaven, and he is met by St Peter.

"Welcome," says St Peter. "Unfortunately there's a slight problem. We seldom see politicians up here, so we're not sure what to do with you."

"No problem," says the politician, "just let me in."

"I'd like to, but I have orders from 'on high.' You need to spend a day in hell, and a day in heaven. Then you can choose where to spend eternity."

"Oh no need, I want to be in heaven," says the politician.

"I'm sorry but rules are rules," insists St Peter. And with that, St. Peter escorts the politician to the lift which takes him down to hell. The doors open and he finds himself in the middle of a green golf course. In the distance is a club, and standing in front of it are all his friends and other politicians who'd worked with him. Everyone is happy and they run to greet him, shake his hand, and reminisce about the good times. They play a great game of golf and then dine on crayfish, caviar and champagne. Also present is the devil, who's very friendly and funny. They're all having such a good time that, before he realises, it's time to go. Everyone gives the politician a hearty farewell and wave while the lift takes him on its upward journey. It goes all the way to heaven, where St Peter is waiting.

"Now it's time for you to visit heaven." So the pollie joins a group of contented souls, moving from cloud to cloud playing the harp and, before he realizes it, the 24 hours have gone by, and St. Peter returns.

"You've spent a day in hell and a day in heaven. Now choose for eternity."

The politician reflects for a minute, then answers, "Well heaven has been delightful, but I'm surprised to say that I'd be better off in hell." So, St Peter escorts him to the lift and the politician goes down, down, down to hell.

The lift doors open, and he finds he's in the middle of a barren land covered with waste and debris. He sees all his friends, but this time dressed in rags, picking up rubbish and putting it in bags. The Devil comes over to him and puts his arm around his shoulder.

"I don't understand," stammers the pollie.

"Yesterday there was a golf course and a club, we ate crayfish and caviar, drank champagne and had a great time. Now there's nothing but a wasteland full of garbage, and my friends look miserable. What happened?"

The Devil looks at him, smiles and says, "Yesterday we were campaigning; today you voted…"

PSYCHOLOGY

A study conducted by the University Department of Psychiatry has revealed that the kind of face a woman finds attractive on a man can differ depending on where she is in her menstrual cycle.

If she is ovulating, she is attracted to men with rugged and masculine features.

But, if she is menstruating or menopausal, she tends to be more attracted to a man with duct tape over his mouth and a spear lodged in his chest while he's on fire. No further studies are expected.

★

A psychiatrist was holding group therapy with four young mothers and their small children.

To the first, he said: "You are obsessed with eating – you even named your daughter Candy."

To the second: "Your obsession is money, your daughter's called Penny."

To the third: "You're obsessed with alcohol. Your child's called Brandy."

At this point, the fourth got up, took her son's hand and whispered: "Come on, Dick, we're going. Let's pick Willy up from school and go home."

RELIGIOUS

A vicar decided to emphasise the point of his sermon with props. He placed four worms in four separate jars. The first worm was placed in a container of alcohol. The second in a container of cigarette smoke.

The third in a container of chocolate syrup. The fourth in a container of good clean soil.

At the end of the sermon, the vicar displayed the four containers showing that the first worm in alcohol was dead. The second in cigarette smoke was also dead. As was the third in chocolate syrup. But the fourth worm in good clean soil was alive.

"What can you learn from this?" the vicar asked.

Bert quickly raised his hand and calls out, "As long as you drink, smoke and eat chocolate, you won't have worms!"

RELIGIOUS LEADERS

A minister was a passionate golfer, usually playing at least one round each week. He strongly believed that Christians should not play sport on Sundays.

But one week, he was too busy to play except on Sunday afternoon. So he fell to temptation and decided to play then. An angel seeing the sin told God. God told the angel that the minister would be punished. Meanwhile on the first hole, the pastor hit a hole in one. Then he did this on the second and the third. The angel flew to God and reminded Him that He said He would punish the pastor. God replied: "Who is the pastor going to tell?"

★

A priest, a Pentecostal preacher, and a rabbi all served as chaplains to the students at the University of Alaska.

They met two or three times a week for coffee and a chat. One day, someone made the comment that preaching to people isn't really all that hard. A real challenge would be to preach to a bear. One thing led to another and they decided to do an experiment. They would all go out into the woods, find a bear, preach to it, and attempt to convert it.

Seven days later, they all came together to discuss their experience.

Father Flannery, who had his arm in a sling, was on crutches and had various bandages on his body and limbs, went first. "Well," he said, "I went into the woods to find a bear. And when I found him I began to read to him from the catechism. Well, that bear wanted nothing to do with me and began to slap me around. So I quickly grabbed my holy water, sprinkled him and, he became gentle as a lamb. The bishop is coming out next week to give him first communion and confirmation."

Reverend Billy Dexter spoke next. He was in a wheelchair, with an IV drip in his arm and both legs in casts. In his best fire and brimstone oratory he boomed, "Well, brothers, you know that we don't sprinkle! I went out and I found a bear. And then I began to read to my bear from God's holy word! But that bear wanted nothing to do with me. So I took hold of him and we began to wrestle. We wrestled down one hill, up another and down another until we came to a creek. So I quickly dunked him and baptised his hairy soul. And just like you said, he became as gentle as a lamb. We spent the rest of the day praising Jesus."

The priest and the reverend both looked down at the rabbi, who was lying in a hospital bed. He was in a body cast and in traction, with monitors, and tubes running in and out of him. He was in real bad shape.

The rabbi looked up and said, "In retrospect, circumcision may not have been the best way to start..."

RETIREMENT

Working people frequently ask retired people what they do to make their days interesting. Well, for example, the other day my wife and I went into town and went into a shop. We were only in there for about 5 minutes. When we came out, there was a policeman writing out a parking ticket.

We went up to him and said, "Come on man, how about giving a senior citizen a break?"

He ignored us and continued writing the ticket. I called him a Nazi turd. He glared at me and started writing another ticket for having worn tyres. So my wife called him a drongo. He finished the second ticket and put it on the windscreen with the first. Then he started writing a third ticket. This went on for about 20 minutes. The more we abused him, the more tickets he wrote.

Personally, we didn't care. We try to have a little fun each day now that we're retired. It's important at our age. Oh, and we came into town by bus!

★

One day, while going to the shops, I passed a nursing home. On the front lawn were six old ladies lying naked on the grass. I thought this a bit unusual, but continued on my way. On my return, I passed the same nursing home with the same six old ladies lying naked on the lawn.

This time my curiosity got the better of me, and I went inside to talk to the Nursing Home Administrator. "Do you know that six ladies are lying naked on your front lawn?"

"Yes," she said. "They're retired prostitutes - they're having a garage sale."

REVENGE

Jake was dying. His wife sat at the bedside. He looked up and said weakly, "I have something I must confess."

"There's no need to," his wife replied.

"No," he insisted, "I want to die in peace. I slept with your sister, your best friend, her best friend, and your mother!"

"I know," she replied, "now just rest and let the poison work."

★

A wife comes home late at night, and quietly opens the door to her bedroom. From under the blanket she sees four legs instead of two.

She reaches for a baseball bat and starts hitting the blanket as hard as she can. Leaving the covered bodies groaning, she goes to the kitchen to have a drink.

As she enters, she sees her husband there, reading a magazine.

"Hi darling," he says, "Your parents have come to visit, so I let them stay in our bedroom. Did you say hello?"

★

A jogger was on his daily run when he saw a strange funeral procession. A hearse was followed closely by another hearse. Walking behind the second hearse was a man with his German Shepherd on a leash. Behind them were about 100 men walking solemnly in single file.

The jogger couldn't restrain his curiosity. He approached the man walking the dog and said: "I'm sorry for your loss, and I hope you don't mind me saying that I've never seen a funeral like this. Whose funeral is it?"

"My wife's."

"What happened to her?"

"She screamed at me and my dog attacked and killed her."

"But who's in the second hearse?" The husband answered, "My mother-in-law. She was trying to help my wife when the dog turned on her."

A very heartfelt moment of brotherhood passed between the two men. Then the jogger asked, "Can I borrow the dog?"

The husband replied, "Join the queue."

★

Fred is watching television when his wife, Sally, rushes up to him and hits him on the head with a saucepan.

"What did you do that for?" Fred shouts, holding his sore head.

"That was for the piece of paper in your pants pocket, with the name Daisy May written on it," Sally replies.

"That's the name of one of the dogs I bet on when I went to the races last Saturday," Fred says.

Sally gasps and apologises.

The next evening Fred is again watching television when Sally flies in and hits him with the pressure cooker and knocks him unconscious. When he revives Fred whispers, "What was that for?"

"Your dog rang."

RUSSIAN

A plane from England to Russia passes through a severe storm.

The turbulence is awful, and things go from bad to worse when one wing is struck by lightning.

One woman, in particular, loses it. Screaming, she stands up in the front of the plane.

"I'm too young to die," she screams.

Then she yells, "If I'm going to die, I want my last minutes on earth to be memorable! Is there anyone on this plane who can make me feel like a WOMAN?"

For a moment there is silence. Everyone has forgotten their own peril.

They all stare, eyes riveted, at this desperate woman in the front of the plane.

Then a Russian stands up in the rear of the plane.

He is handsome, muscular, with blonde hair and blue eyes.

He starts to walk slowly up the aisle, while unbuttoning his shirt, one button at a time.

No one moves. He removes his shirt. Muscles ripple across his chest.

She gasps. He whispers, "Iron zis. Zen get me a vodka."

SALES

A young Aussie bloke moved to London and went to Harrods looking for a job. The manager asked "Do you have any sales experience young man?"

The young man answered, "Yeah, I was a salesman back home in Melbourne."

The manager liked the Aussie so he gave him the job. His first day on the job was challenging and busy, but he got through it.

After the store was locked up, the manager came down and asked, "How many sales did you make today?"

The Aussie said, "One!"

The manager groaned and continued, "Just one? Our sales people average 20 or 30 sales a day. How much was the sale for?"

"£124,237.64."

The manager choked and exclaimed "£124,237.64!! What on earth did you sell?"

"Well, first I sold the customer a small fish hook, then a medium fish hook and then I sold him a new fishing rod. Then I asked him where he was going fishing and he said down at the coast, so I told him he would need a boat, so we went down to the boat department and I sold him that twin-engine Power Cat. Then he said he didn't think his Honda Civic would pull it, so I took him down to car sales and I sold him the 4WD Range Rover."

The manager, incredulous, said "You mean to tell me, a guy came in here to buy a fish hook and you sold him a boat and a 4WD?"

"No no no... he came in here to buy a box of tampons for his wife and I said... 'Well, since your weekend's ruined, you might as well go fishing.'"

★

An old lady answered a knock on the door one day, to a well-dressed young man carrying a vacuum cleaner.

"Good morning," said the young man. "Could I take a couple of minutes of your time to demonstrate the very latest in high-powered vacuum cleaners?"

"Go away!" said the old lady. "I'm broke!" and she proceeded to close the door.

Quick as a flash, the young man wedged his foot in the door and pushed it wide open.

"Don't be too hasty!" he said. "Not until you have at least

seen my demonstration."

And with that, he emptied a bucket of horse manure onto her hall carpet.

"Now; if this vacuum cleaner does not remove all traces of this horse manure from your carpet, madam, I will personally eat the remainder."

The old lady stepped back and said, "Well let me get you a spoon, 'cause they cut off my electricity this morning."

SCHOOL

The teacher Miss Harris points to a map hanging on the wall and asks Jane to, "Go to the map and find Australia."

"Here it is," points Jane.

"That's right," says Miss Harris. "Now class, who discovered Australia?"

"Jane!" the class choruses.

★

Teacher: "Charlie, how do you spell kangaroo?"
Charlie: "C A N G A R U."
Teacher: "No Charlie, that's wrong."
Charlie: "It might be wrong but you asked me how I spelt it"

★

Teacher: "Richard, what is water's chemical formula?"
Richard: "H I J K L M N O"
Teacher: "Richard, what are you saying?"
Richard: "But Miss yesterday you said it was H to O."

★

Teacher: "Bill, name one important thing we have today that we didn't have 10 years ago."

Bill. "Me!"

★

The school inspector is assigned to the fourth grade in a Brisbane State School. He's introduced to the class by the teacher. She says, "Let's show the inspector just how clever you are by answering his question."

The inspector reasons that normally class starts with religious instruction, so he asks a Biblical question. "Class, who broke down the walls of Jericho?"

For a full minute there is complete silence. The children all stare at him blankly. Eventually Bruce raises his hand. The inspector excitedly points to him.

Bruce stands up and replies, "Sir, I don't know who broke down the walls of Jericho, but it wasn't me."

The inspector is shocked by the answer and the lack of knowledge of the famous Bible story and he looks at the teacher for an explanation. The teacher says, "I've known Bruce since the beginning of the year, and I believe that if he says he didn't do it, then he didn't."

The inspector is flabbergasted and storms to the principal's office and tells him what happened, to which the principal replies, "I don't know the boy, but I socialize every now and then with his teacher, and I believe her. If she feels that the boy is innocent, then he must be innocent."

The inspector can't believe what he's hearing. He grabs the 'phone on the principal's desk and in a rage, dials the Minister of Education's telephone number, rattles off the entire occurrence to her and asks her what she thinks of the educational standard in the State.

The Minister sighs heavily and replies, "I don't know the boy, the teacher or the principal, but just get three quotes and have the wall fixed!"

★

Teacher: "Tom what do you call someone who keeps talking to people even when they're no longer interested?"

Tom: "A teacher."

SCOTTISH

A Scottish woman goes to the local newspaper office to see that the obituary for her recently deceased husband is published.

The obituary editor tells her that there is a charge of 50 cents per word.

She pauses, reflects, and then says, "Well, let it read, 'Angus MacPherson died'."

Amused at the woman's thrift, the editor tells her that there is a seven word minimum for all obituaries.

She thinks it over and in a few seconds says, "In that case, let it read, 'Angus MacPherson died. Golf clubs for sale'."

★

A young Scottish lad and lass were sitting on a low stone wall, holding hands, gazing out over the loch. For several minutes they sat silently.

Then finally the girl looked at the boy and said, "A penny for your thoughts, Hamish."

"Well, uh, I was thinkin'... perhaps it's aboot time for a wee kiss."

The girl blushed, then leaned over and kissed him lightly on the cheek. Then he blushed. The two turned once again to gaze out over the loch.

Minutes passed and the girl spoke again. "Another penny for your thoughts, Hamish."

"Well, uh, I was thinkin' perhaps it's aboot time for a wee cuddle."

The girl blushed, then leaned over and cuddled him for a few seconds. Then he blushed. And the two turned once again to gaze out over the loch.

After a while, she again said, "Another penny for your thoughts, Hamish."

"Well, uh, I was thinkin' perhaps it's aboot time you let me put my hand on your leg."

The girl blushed, then took his hand and put it on her knee. Then he blushed. Then the two turned once again to gaze out over the loch before the girl spoke again.

"Another penny for your thoughts, Hamish." The young man glanced down with a furrowed brow.

"Well, noo," he said, "my thoughts are a wee bit more serious this time."

"Really?" said the lass in a whisper, filled with anticipation.

"Aye," said the lad, nodding.

The girl looked away in shyness, began to blush, and bit her lip in anticipation of the ultimate request. Then he said, "Dae ye nae think it's aboot time ye paid me the pennies?"

★

An Arab Sheik was admitted to St Vincent's Hospital for heart surgery, but before surgery, the doctors had to store blood in case a need arose. As the gentleman had a rare blood type, it couldn't be found locally, and the call went out to all the states.

Finally, a Scot was found who had a similar blood type. The Scot willingly donated his blood for the Arab. The Arab was so grateful that he wasted no time and even before the surgery, gave instructions for the Scotsman to be sent a new BMW and diamonds in appreciation of his generosity.

A couple of days later, the Arab had to go through a corrective surgery. His doctor telephoned the Scotsman who was more than happy to donate his blood again.

After the second surgery, the Arab sent the Scotsman a thank-you card and a jar of lollies.

The Scotsman was shocked that the Arab did not reciprocate his kind gesture as generously as the first time. He 'phoned the Arab and said, "I thought you would be as generous again, after giving me a BMW and diamonds. But you only gave me a thank-you card and a jar of lollies. Why?"

To this the Arab replied, "Aye, but I now have Scottish blood in me veins."

★

Three couples are enjoying a round of golf together. The French wife Yvette, steps up to the tee and as she bends over to place her ball, a gust of wind blows her skirt up and reveals her lack of underwear.

"Pour l'amour de Dieu, Yvette! Vy aren't you vearing any scanties," husband Pierre shouts.

"Vell, you don't give me enoff housekeeping monee to buy any."

Pierre immediately takes out his wallet and draws out a

---

note saying, "Pleeze for your reputation buy undervear as soon as posseeble."

Then the English wife Brenda, bends over to set her ball on the tee. Her skirt also blows up to reveal no underwear.

"For goodness sake Brenda," shrieks husband Albert. "You're not wearing any drawers. Why?"

"With the pittance you give me for housekeeping, I've not got enough for such luxuries," she says. Bert gives her a note. "For the sake of decency, here's some money to buy some."

Lastly, the Scotsman's wife bends over. The wind also takes her skirt over her head to reveal that she, too, is naked under it.

"Aggie! Where the frig are yer drawers?"

She too explains, "You din na give me enough money ta be able ta affarrd any."

The Scotsman reaches into his pocket and says, "Well, fer the love 'o decency, here's a comb... Tidy yerself up a bit."

SENIOR ROMANCE

Bob, a 70 year old, extremely wealthy widower, shows up at the Country Club with a breathtakingly beautiful and sexy 25 year old blonde, who hangs over Bob's arm and listens intently to his every word. His mates at the club are all gobsmacked.

At the first chance, they corner him and ask, "Bob, how'd you get the trophy girlfriend?"

Bob replies, "Girlfriend? She's my wife!"

They're staggered, but continue. "What? How'd you persuade her to marry you?"

"I lied about my age," Bob smiled.

"Did you tell her you were only 50?"

"No, I told her I was 90."

★

Jane popped in to welcome her new neighbours at the retirement village and was invited to stay for a cup of tea. She was very impressed how the hostess Betty preceded every request to her husband with endearing terms such as: Honey, My love, Darling, Sweetheart, Pumpkin, etc. The couple had been married almost 70 years and, clearly, they were still very much in love.

When the husband went outside to water the plants, Jane said to Betty, "I think it's wonderful that, after all these years, you still call your husband all those loving pet names."

Betty hung her head. "I must tell you the truth," she said. "His name slipped my mind about 10 years ago, and I'm scared to death to ask the grumpy old man what his name is."

SENIOR SEX

One night an 87 year old woman came home from Bingo to find her 92 year old husband in bed with another woman. She couldn't control her emotions and pushed him off the balcony of their 5th floor "assisted living apartment" – killing him instantly.

Brought before the court on the charge of murder, the judge asked her if she had anything to say in her defence.

She began coolly. "Yes, your honour, I reckoned that at 92, if he could have sex, he could fly."

★

An elderly man goes into a brothel and tells the madam he would like a young girl for the night. Surprised, she looks at the ancient man and asks how old he is.

"I'm 90 years old," he says.

"90?" replies the woman. "Don't you realize you've had it?"

"Oh, sorry," says the old man. "How much do I owe you?"

★

An elderly couple had been married for umpteen years and normally each went to sleep early, but this evening the wife was in a romantic mood...

The husband wanted to sleep, but she said, "You used to hold my hand when we were courting."

Wearily he reached across, held her hand for a second and then tried to get back to sleep.

A few moments later she said, "Then you used to kiss me."

Mildly irritated, he reached across, gave her a peck on the cheek and settled down to sleep.

Thirty seconds later she said, "Then you used to bite my neck."

Angrily, he threw back the bed clothes and got out of bed.

"Where are you going?" She asked.

"To get my teeth!"

SEX

A young man called Ben boarded an aircraft at Melbourne Airport for Paris, when he couldn't believe his luck. A gorgeous woman sat down beside him.

"Hi," he greeted her warmly, "Are you on a business trip or on a holiday?"

She smiled and replied, "Business. I'm going to a

nymphomaniac conference in Paris."

Ben gulped. Was he dreaming? This gorgeous woman beside him was a nymphomaniac!

Controlling his emotions he asked quietly, "What's your role at this conference?"

"I'm presenting a paper," she replied. "I use my personal experience to expose some misconceptions about sexuality."

"Oh?" He replied, finding it hard to breathe quietly. "What are they?"

"For instance one myth is that African negroes are the most well-endowed, when, in fact, it's the Maoris who head the list. Another misconception is that Italians are the best lovers, when it's the Spanish. The best potential lovers are the Russians."

Just then she stopped abruptly and her face turned a delicate pink. "Oh, please forgive me. I shouldn't be discussing this with you. I don't even know your name."

"Arapeta Almaraz," Ben said, "but my friends call me Ivan."

★

A woman sees a man travelling with 16 children.

"Are all these kids yours?" she asks.

The man replies, "No, I work in a condom factory and these are customer complaints."

★

A couple agree that whoever died first would come back and tell the other if there is sex after death. Their biggest fear was that there was no after-life at all. After a long life together, the husband was the first to die.

True to his word, he made the first contact, "Glenda... Glenda."

"Is that you, Ted?"

"Yes, I've come back like we agreed."

"That's wonderful! What's it like?"

"Well, I get up in the morning. I have sex. I have breakfast and then it's off to the golf course.

"I have sex again, bathe in the warm sun and then have sex a couple more times.

"Then I have lunch (you'd be proud – lots of greens). Another romp around the golf course, then pretty much have sex the rest of the afternoon.

"After dinner, it's back to the golf course again.

"Then it's more sex until late at night. I catch some much-needed sleep and then the next day it starts all over again."

"Oh, Ted... are you in Heaven?"

"No... I'm a rabbit in Ballarat."

SPORT

A Scotsman moves to Canada and attends his first baseball game.

The first batter approaches the batter's box, takes a few swings and then hits a double. Everyone is on their feet screaming, "RUN."

The next batter hits a single. The Scotsman listens as the crowd again cheers, "RUN RUN." The Scotsman is enjoying the game and begins screaming with the fans.

The third batter comes up and four balls go by. The Umpire calls, "Walk."

The batter starts his slow trot to first base. The Scot stands up and screams, "Run ye bampot, RRUNN!"

The people around him begin laughing. Embarrassed, the

Scot sits down. A friendly fan notes the man's embarrassment, leans over and explains, "He can't run -- he's got four balls."

The Scot stands up and screams, "Walk with pride, Laddie!"

SPRUNG

Carol was having a passionate affair with Derek an inspector from a pest-control company. One afternoon they were making love in the bedroom when her husband Trevor arrived home unexpectedly.

"Quick," said Carol, "into the wardrobe!" and she pushed Derek into the wardrobe, stark naked.

Trevor on discovering his dishevelled wife, became suspicious and after searching the bedroom discovered Derek in the wardrobe.

"Who are you?" he asked.

"I'm an inspector from Bugs-B-Gone," said the exterminator.

"What are you doing in there?" Trevor asked.

"I'm investigating a complaint about an infestation of clothes moths," Derek replied.

"'And where are your clothes?" asked Trevor.

Derek looked down at himself and said, "Those little ba...s!!"

SUICIDE

Agnes at 91 was grieving the recent death of George, her husband of more than 70 years. She decided to kill herself and reunite with him.

She found George's old army pistol and decided to shoot

herself in the heart, since it was already badly broken.

Not wanting to miss the vital organ and become a vegetable and a burden to her family; she called her doctor to ask where exactly would the heart be on a woman. The doctor said, "Your heart is just below your left breast."

Later that day Agnes was admitted to hospital – with a gunshot wound to her knee!

SUNDAY SCHOOL

At Sunday School, little Jimmy was listening to the Bible story about Lot. The teacher read, "Lot was warned to take his wife and flee out of the city but his wife looked back and was turned to salt."

Concerned, little Jimmy asked, "What happened to the flea?"

★

A Sunday School teacher was looking at the children's pictures while they were drawing. She asked one little girl Sally, who was working diligently, to explain her picture.

Sally replied, "I'm drawing God."

The teacher quietly replied, "No one really knows what God looks like."

Sally replied, "They will when I've finished."

★

A Sunday school teacher asked, "Johnny, do you think Noah did a lot of fishing when he was on the Ark ?"

"No," replied Johnny. "How could he, with just two worms."

TECHNOLOGY

A little boy goes up to his father and asks, "Daddy, how was I born?"

"Well, son," the father replies," your mum and I first got together in a chat room on Google. I then set up a date via email with your mum and we met at a cybercafé. We sneaked off into a secluded room and activated my hard drive. We then discovered that neither of us had used a firewall and it was too late to hit the delete button. Anyway, nine months later a blessed little pop-up appeared. It read, 'You've got male'."

★

A Montana couple decided to go to Florida to escape the icy winter. They planned to stay at the hotel, where they had spent their honeymoon, 20 years before. Because of hectic schedules, it was difficult to coordinate their travel times. So, the husband left Montana and flew to Florida on Friday and his wife was to join him the following day.

The husband checked into the hotel. There was a computer in his room, so he decided to send an email to his wife. However, he accidentally left out one letter in her email address, and without realizing his mistake, sent the email.

Meanwhile, somewhere in Montana, a widow had just returned home from her husband's funeral. He was a minister who was called home to glory following a heart attack. The widow decided to check her email expecting messages from relatives and friends. After reading the first message, she fainted. The widow's son rushed into the room, found his mother on the floor, and saw the computer screen which read,

To: My Loving Wife
Subject: I've Arrived
Date: October 16, 2000

I know you're surprised to hear from me. They have computers here now and you're allowed to send emails to your loved ones. I've just arrived and have been checked in. I see that everything has been prepared for your arrival tomorrow. Looking forward to seeing you then! Hope your journey is as uneventful as mine was.

P. S. Sure is hot down here.

★

A young executive was leaving the office late one evening when he found the CEO standing in front of a shredder with a piece of paper in his hand.

"Listen," said the CEO, "this is a very sensitive and important document, and my secretary has gone for the night. Can you make this thing work?"

"Certainly," said the young executive. He turned the machine on, inserted the paper, and pressed the start button.

"Excellent, excellent!" said the CEO as his paper disappeared inside the machine, "I only need one copy."

TERRORISM

After much publicity about the US not knowing whether Osama Bin Laden was still alive, Osama decided to send George Bush a letter in his own handwriting to let him know he was still a threat. Bush opened the letter and it appeared to contain a single line of coded message: 370H-SSV-0773H.

Bush was puzzled, so he emailed it to his secretary of state, Condoleeza Rice. Rice and her aides had no idea what it meant either, so they sent it to the FBI.

No one could solve it at the FBI so it went to the CIA, then to NASA. Eventually they asked Australia's ASIO for help. Within minutes ASIO cabled the White House with this reply. "Tell the President he's holding the message upside down..."

★

I was so depressed last night thinking about the economy, wars, jobs, my savings, Social Security, etc., I called the Suicide Hotline. I got a call centre in Pakistan, and when I told them I was suicidal, they got all excited, and asked if I could drive a truck.

TODDLERS

One afternoon while Jenny was out shopping, husband Mark was left to look after their two year old daughter Ella. She'd received a doll's tea set for her second birthday, which was one of her favourite toys.

Mark was in the living room watching the footy when Ella brought him a little cup of 'tea', (water). After several cups of tea and lots of praise for such yummy tea, Jenny returned home.

Mark greeted Jenny saying, "You've got to watch this cute game Ella and I have been playing!"

Jenny watched as Ella came in with a cup of 'tea' for 'Daddy' and watched Mark drink it. Then she said, "You do realise that the only place Ella can reach to get water is the toilet bowl?"

TRAVEL

A young Melbourne woman was so depressed that she decided to end her life by throwing herself into the sea, but just before she threw herself from the wharf, a handsome young man stopped her.

"You have so much to live for," said the man. "I'm a sailor, and we're off to France tomorrow. I can stow you away on my ship. I'll take care of you, bring you food every day, and keep you happy."

With nothing to lose, combined with the fact that she had always wanted to go to France, the woman accepted.

That night the sailor brought her aboard and hid her in a small but comfortable compartment in the hold. From then on, every night he would bring her sandwiches, a bottle of red wine, and make love to her until dawn. Two weeks later she was discovered by the captain during a routine inspection.

"What are you doing here?" asked the captain.

"I have an arrangement with one of the sailors," she replied. "He brings me food and I get a free trip to France."

"I see," the captain said.

The woman's conscience got the best of her and she added, "Plus, he's screwing me."

"He certainly is," replied the captain. "This is the Tasmanian Ferry."

UNIONS

Melburnian Geoff was attending a union conference in Sydney. On his night off he decided to meet some girls at Kings Cross. But being dedicated to fair work conditions, he was only interested in brothels that gave their girls a fair deal.

At the first one, Geoff asked the Madam, "Are you registered with a union?"

"No sir, we're not," she replied.

"If I paid you $100, what cut would the girl get?"

"The house gets $80 and the girls get $20," she answered.

Offended at such unfair dealings, the unionist stomped off down the street in search of a more equitable, hopefully unionized brothel. Finally, he found a brothel where the Madam responded, "Why yes, this is a union house. We observe all union rules."

Geoff asked, "And, if I paid you $100, what cut do the girls get?"

"The girls get $80 and the house gets $20."

"That's more like it!" Geoff said. He handed the Madam $100, looked around the room, and pointed to a stunningly attractive green-eyed blonde.

"I'd like her," he said.

"I'm sure you would, sir," said the Madam. Then she gestured to an 82 year old woman in the corner, "but Ethel here has 62 years seniority and according to union rules, she's next!"

VANITY

I was sitting in the waiting room for my first appointment with a new dentist. On the wall was his dental diploma, with his full name. It brought back memories of a tall handsome dark-haired boy with the same name in my secondary school class about 35 years ago.

Could he be the same person that I had a secret crush on all those years ago?

On seeing him, I quickly dropped that thought. This balding, grey haired man with the deeply lined face was far too old to have been my classmate. But after he examined my teeth I asked him anyway if he'd attended Burwood High School.

"Yes I did," he smiled.

"When did you leave?" I asked.

It was the same year that I'd left!

"You were in my class!" I exclaimed.

He looked at me closely. Then that ugly, old, balding, wrinkled, decrepit, drongo asked, "What did you teach?"

★

A 45 year old woman had a heart attack and was taken to the hospital. While on the operating table, she had a near-death experience. Seeing God, she asked "Is my time up?"

God said, "No, you have another 41 years, 5 months and 6 days to live."

On recovery, the woman thought as she had so much more time to live, she might as well make the most of it. So she stayed in the hospital, and had a face-lift, liposuction, breast implants and a tummy tuck. After her last operation, she was released from the hospital. While crossing the street on her way home, she was killed by an ambulance. Arriving in front of God, she demanded, "You said I had another 41 years, 5 months and 6 days to live. Why did you let me die?"

God replied, "I didn't recognize you."

VETS

A man takes his Siberian Husky to the vet. "My dog's cross-eyed, is there anything you can do for him?"

"Well," says the vet, "let's have a look at him."

So he picks the dog up and examines his eyes, then sighs. Finally, he says, "I'm going to have to put him down."

"What? Because he's cross-eyed?"

"No, because he's really heavy."

WEDDINGS

Jacob, aged 92, and Henrietta, aged 89, are excited about their decision to marry. They go for a stroll to discuss the wedding and on the way they pass a chemist. Jacob suggests they go in. Jacob tells the chemist, "We're about to marry. Do you sell heart medication?"

Chemist: "Of course we do."

Jacob: "How about medicine for circulation?"

Chemist: "All kinds."

Jacob: "Medicine for rheumatism, scoliosis?"

Chemist: "Yes."

Jacob: "Medicine for memory problems, arthritis, jaundices?"

Chemist: "Yes, a large variety... the works!"

Jacob: "What about vitamins, sleeping pills, antidotes for Parkinson's Disease?"

Chemist: "Absolutely."

Jacob:"You sell wheelchairs and walkers?"

Chemist: "All speeds and sizes. Why do you ask? Is there something I can help you with?"

Jacob says to the pharmacist: "We'd like to nominate your store as our Bridal Gift Shop."

★

Sam, who is eight, asks his mother, "Why are wedding dresses white?"

Belinda replies, "Sam, this shows friends and relatives that the bride is pure."

Sam thanks his mother but doesn't quite understand her so he asks his father, Bert. "Dad why are wedding dresses white?"

Bert looks at his son in surprise and says, "Sam, all household appliances come in white."

WELSH

A couple at an art exhibition look at a painting that they find puzzling. The picture depicts three very black, very naked men sitting on a park bench; two have black private parts and the one in the middle has pink private parts.

As the couple look somewhat puzzled, the artist walks by and says, "Can I help you with this painting? I painted it."

The man says, "We like the painting but don't understand why you have three African men on a bench, and the one in the middle has pink private parts, while the other two have black private parts."

The artist says, "Oh you're misinterpreting the painting.

"They're not African men, they're Welsh coal miners and the one in the middle went home for lunch."

WISDOM

A woman in a supermarket is following a grandfather and his badly behaved 3 year old grandson. It's obvious to her that the grandfather has his hands full with the child screaming for sweets in the sweet aisle, biscuits in the biscuit aisle, and for fruit, cereal and soft drinks in the other aisles. Meanwhile, Gramps is working his way around, saying in a controlled voice, "Easy, William, we won't be long... easy, boy."

Another outburst, and she hears Gramps calmly say, "It's okay, William, just a couple more minutes and we'll be out of here. Hang in there, boy."

At the checkout, the little terror is throwing items out of the cart, and Gramps says again in a controlled voice, "William, William, relax buddy, don't get upset. We'll be home in five minutes; stay cool, William."

Very impressed, the woman goes outside where the grandfather is loading his groceries and the boy into the car. She says to the elderly man, "It's none of my business, but you were amazing in there. I don't know how you did it. That whole time, you kept your composure, and no matter how loud and disruptive he got, you just calmly kept saying things would be okay. William is very lucky to have you as his grandpa."

"Thanks," said the grandfather, "but I'm William... the little so and so's name is Kevin."

WIVES

Bert died. His will provided $40,000 for an elaborate funeral. As the last guests departed, his widow Pat turned to her oldest and dearest friend.

"Ah well, Bert would be pleased," she said.

"You're right," replied Frances, who lowered her voice and leaned in close.

"So go on, how much did this really cost?"

"All of it," said Pat.

"$40,000."

"No!" Frances exclaimed, "I mean, it was very grand, but $40,000?"

Pat answered, "The funeral was $6,500. I donated $500 to the church. The whisky, wine and finger food were another $500. The rest went for the Memorial Stone."

Frances computed quickly. "For the love of God Pat, $32,500 for a Memorial Stone? How big is it?"

"Take a look," said Pat as she held out her hand to display her new enormous diamond ring!

★

When everybody on earth was dead and waiting to enter Heaven, God appeared and said, "I want the men to make two lines: one line for the men who were true heads of their household, and the other line for the men who were dominated by their women."

Soon, there were two lines of men. The line of the men who were dominated by their wives was 100 kms long, and in the line of men who were true heads of their household, there was only one man.

God said to the long line, "You men should be ashamed of yourselves; I created you to be the head of your household! You have been disobedient and have not fulfilled your purpose! Of all of you, only one obeyed. Learn from him."

God turned to the one man, "How did you manage to be the only one in this line?" The man replied, "My wife told me to stand here."

★

Ralph returns from the doctor and tells his wife Eileen, that the doctor has told him he has only 24 hours to live. Given this prognosis, Ralph asks Eileen for sex. Naturally, she agrees, and they make love. About six hours later, Ralph says to Eileen, "Dear, you know I now only have 18 hours to live. Could we please do it one more time?"

Of course, Eileen agrees and they do it again. Later as Ralph gets into bed, he looks at his watch and realizes he now has only eight hours left. He touches his wife's shoulder and asks, "Dear, please - just one more time, before I die?"

She says, "Of course." And they make love for the third time.

Then Eileen rolls over and falls asleep. Ralph, however, worries about his impending death, tosses and turns until he's down to four more hours. He taps Eileen, who rouses. "Dear, I have only four more hours. Do you think we could....?"

At this point Eilleen rolls over and says, "Listen Ralph, I have to get up in the morning... you don't."

WOMEN'S LIBERATION

A 90 year old women's libber was so incensed that a social club was barred to women that she threw off her clothes and streaked through the lounge. Two men were having a quiet drink there when one said to the other, "George was that a woman running through the lounge just now?"

George said, "Cuthbert I'm not sure what it was, but whatever it was, it needed a good ironing."

WORKERS

Barbara desperately needed a break from work, but she had no leave so she thought if she acted 'crazy' then her boss might insist on her taking time off work.

So Barbara hung upside-down from the ceiling and made funny noises.

Her work mate Anne asked what she was doing, so Barbara explained her plan.

When the Boss came into the office and asked, "What on earth are you doing?" Barbara said that she was a light bulb.

He said, "You're obviously stressed. Go home and rest for a couple of days."

So Barbara jumped down and left the office.

When Anne followed Barbara the Boss asked, "Where do you think you're going?"

Anne replied, "I'm going home, too. I can't work in the dark."

★

I was really pleased to land a part-time job at the local restaurant.

I had to greet customers and direct those first in line to a table as it became available.

At lunchtime on the first day a very loud, mean woman stood in line with her children, swearing at them so they dared not do anything but cower beside her. Mindful of my training I greeted them. But before I knew it I followed it up with, "What sweet twins you have."

The woman looked at me in disdain and bellowed, "No, Stupid. One is 10 and the other is six. What the hell makes you think they're twins?"

So I answered (in my greeter's voice), "I'm not stupid, Madam, but I couldn't believe someone slept with you twice. Have a good day."

I'm now looking for another job.

★

A motorcycle mechanic was removing a cylinder head from the motor of a BMW when he spotted a well-known cardiologist in his shop.

The cardiologist was there waiting for the service manager to come and take a look at his car when the mechanic shouted across the garage, "Hey Doc, want to take a look at this?" The cardiologist, a bit surprised walked over to where the mechanic was working on the motorcycle.

The mechanic straightened up, wiped his hands on a rag and asked, "So Doc, look at this engine. I opened its heart, took the valves out, repaired or replaced anything damaged, and then put everything back in, and when I finished, it worked just like new. So how is that I make $74,000 a year and you make $2M when you and I are doing basically the same work?"

The cardiologist paused, leaned over, and then whispered to the mechanic...

"Try doing it with the engine running."

★

A priest, a doctor, and an engineer were waiting one morning for a particularly slow group of golfers. The engineer fumed, "What's with those guys? We must have been waiting for 15 minutes!"

The doctor chimed in, "I don't know, but I've never seen such inept golf!"

The priest said, "Here comes the greens-keeper. Let's have a word with him." He called out, "Hello George. What's wrong with that group ahead of us? They're rather slow, aren't they?" The greens-keeper replied, "Oh, yes. That's a group of blind firemen. They lost their sight saving our clubhouse from a fire last year, so we always let them play for free!"

The group fell silent for a moment. The priest said, "That's so sad. I think I will say a special prayer for them tonight."

The doctor said, "Good idea. I'm going to contact my ophthalmologist colleague and see if there's anything she can do for them."

The engineer said, "Why can't they play at night?"

YOUNG ROMANCE

Pat asks her boyfriend David to come over one evening to meet her parents, and have dinner with them. Since this is such a big event, Pat says to David that after dinner, she'd like to go out and make love for the first time. David is ecstatic, but he has never had sex before, so he goes to the pharmacist to buy some condoms. He tells the pharmacist it's his first time and the pharmacist helps David for about an hour. He tells David everything there is to know about condoms and sex.

That night, David arrives at Pat's parents' house and meets her at the door. "Oh, I'm so excited that you're meeting my parents, come on in!"

David enters and is taken to the dinner table where Pat's parents are seated. David quickly offers to say grace and bows his head. A minute passes, and David is still deep in prayer, with his head down.

Five then ten minutes pass, and still no movement from David. Finally Pat leans over and whispers to David, "I had no idea you were this religious."

David whispers back, "I had no idea your father was a pharmacist."

ABOUT THE AUTHOR

Marguerite Marshall lives in Melbourne with husband Robert and has a grown up family. Marguerite is a journalist, having written for publications including *The Age, The Herald, The West Australian* and the *Post Courier* in *PNG*. She authored the history book *Nillumbik Now and Then*. For light relief she loves to share jokes.

BEST AUSSIE JOKES
MARGUERITE MARSHALL

ISBN 9781922175557   Qty

RRP   AU$19.99   .....

Postage within Australia   AU$5.00   .....

TOTAL★ $_____

★ All prices include GST

Name:...

Address: ....

....

Phone:..

Email: ....

Payment: ❑ Money Order ❑ Cheque ❑ MasterCard ❑ Visa

Cardholders Name:...

Credit Card Number: ....

Signature:...

Expiry Date: ....

Allow 7 days for delivery.

Payment to: Marzocco Consultancy (ABN 14 067 257 390)
                        PO Box 12544
                        A'Beckett Street, Melbourne, 8006
                        Victoria, Australia
                        admin@brolgapublishing.com.au

Be Published

Publish through a successful publisher.
Brolga Publishing is represented through:
• **National** book trade distribution, including sales,
marketing & distribution through **Macmillan Australia.**
• **International** book trade distribution to
    • The United Kingdom
    • North America
    • Sales representation in South East Asia
• **Worldwide e-Book distribution**

For details and inquiries, contact:
Brolga Publishing Pty Ltd
PO Box 12544
A'Beckett St VIC 8006

Phone: 0414 608 494
markzocchi@brolgapublishing.com.au
ABN: 46 063 962 443
(Email for a catalogue request)